Also from Robert Barnard

The Killings on Jubilee Terrace

*

ROBERT BARNARD

SCRIBNER

NEW YORK   LONDON   TORONTO   SYDNEY

SCRIBNER
A Division of Simon & Schuster, Inc.
1230 Avenue of the Americas
New York, NY 10020

First Scribner hardcover edition May 2009

SCRIBNER and design are registered trademarks of The Gale Group, Inc.,
used under license by Simon & Schuster, Inc., the publisher of this work.

For information about special discounts for bulk purchases,
please contact Simon & Schuster Special Sales at 1-800-456-6798
or business@simonandschuster.com.

The Simon & Schuster Speakers Bureau can bring authors to your live event.
For more information or to book an event contact the Simon & Schuster Speakers
Bureau at 1-866-248-3049 or visit our website at www.simonspeakers.com.

Manufactured in the United States of America

1   3   5   7   9   10   8   6   4   2

Library of Congress Cataloging-in-Publication Data

Barnard, Robert.
The Killings on Jubilee Terrace : a novel of suspense / Robert
Barnard.—1st Scribner hardcover ed.
p. cm.
1. Television actors and actresses—Fiction.
2. Television soap operas—Fiction. 3. England—Fiction. I. Title.
PR6052.A665K56 2009
823'.914—dc22
2009002377

ISBN-13: 978-1-4165-5942-9
ISBN-10: 1-4165-5942-6

The Killings on
Jubilee Terrace

CHARACTERS AND ACTORS
IN THE TV SOAP OPERA *JUBILEE TERRACE*

CHARACTER	ACTOR
Arthur Bradley, corner shop owner	Garry Kopps
Will Brown, the Terrace's token black	James Selcott
Maureen Cooke, wife of Arthur Bradley	Shirley Merritt
Harry Hornby, newsagent	Les Crosby
Dawn Kerridge, the Terrace's romantic interest	Susan Fyldes
Norma Kerridge, her mother	Carol Chisholm
Peter Kerridge, her father	Philip Marston
Kevin Plunkett, the Terrace's religious interest	Stephen Barrymore
Bert Porter, recently dead Terrace stalwart	Vernon Watts
Gladys Porter, his wife	Marjorie Harcourt-Smith
Rita Somerville, florist	Bet Garrett
Vicar, drunk and disorderly	George Price
Cyril Wharton, the Terrace's token gay	Hamish Fawley
Lady Wharton, his mother	Winnie Hey
Bob Worseley, landlord of the Duke of York's	Bill Garrett
Sally Worseley, his wife	Liza Croome
Jason Worseley, their son	Theodor Mossby (Young Foulmouth)

CHAPTER 1

A Death

✳

"Bert—I'm home," Gladys Porter called up the stairs, when she had let herself into the hallway of her terraced house. "I'll put the kettle on for a nice cup of tea."

She was about to potter through to the kitchen when her face registered that there had been no reply.

"Bert? I said I'd make a nice cup of tea."

Still there was silence from above.

Gladys put down her shopping bag and rushed stumbling up the stairs. Seconds later she was running down them, through the door, and out into Jubilee Terrace, where she fell into the arms of her neighbor Norma Kerridge.

"It's my Bert," she sobbed, her face a picture of distress. "Help me, Norma. I think he's . . . *dead*."

The viewing public, all the nine million who switched on regularly at 7:30 p.m. Monday to Friday, already knew that Bert was dead. Vernon Watts, who for the past ten years had played Bert Porter in *Jubilee Terrace*, had had a heart attack while crossing a road, had been hit by a bus, and had died shortly after in hospital. That was two months ago, in Highgate. Since then he had been written out of the soap, apparently confined to bed with a vague, undisclosed illness. Now, having been written out by the Almighty, he had gone the way ordained by a script conference.

The public had been grieved by Vernon's death. He had once been a comic around the Northern clubs and smaller music halls, and his public image was of a plump, genial man, a bit of a card. St. Stephen's Church in Highgate, where Watts had not worshiped, was ablaze with flowers from his fans, most of them addressed to the fictional Bert Porter. His real-life widow received very little media attention, but his *Jubilee Terrace* widow had been lovingly photographed sobbing as she came out of the church. His real widow did not mind her neglect. She was glad not to have had to pay public tribute to her hated husband.

"He was like a second husband to me," his television widow was quoted as saying to a *Daily Star* reporter.

In the studio canteen, after filming the scene of Bert's demise, Marjorie Harcourt-Smith, who played Gladys, dabbed at her eyes with a little lace handkerchief.

"I've been dreading doing that scene," she said, in her impeccably Mayfair normal voice. "And it was *awful*. Thank God it's in the bag. It was really upsetting."

Carol Chisholm, who played Norma Kerridge the neighbor, sipped at her tea and kept her eyebrows firmly unraised.

"But you and Vernon never really . . . got on, did you?" she said, trying to be tactful.

"I hated Vernon Watts more than anyone in my whole life—barring my husband, God rest his soul. That's beside the point. We had a professional partnership. The fact that we also had a personal guerrilla war is neither here nor there."

It was a distinction Carol Chisholm grasped easily. She nodded her professional understanding.

"Of course it's different with Philip and me. We get on quite well. I don't mean I'm in the least *attracted*, or him to me, or that we'd marry if my husband and his wife died or anything like that. But we do enjoy each other's company. We have a lot of drinks together, as you know, and a lot of laughs. That means that filming the Kerridge family scenes is usually a pleasure."

Marjorie tucked a cigarette into an immensely elegant ivory holder. It was a demonstration against the fact that smoking was now forbidden in the canteen. The gesture was weakened by her failure to light up.

"It's Susan *you* can't abide," she said shrewdly.

"Now that's not fair. We're always perfectly polite to each other. She's still young. There's lots of time for her to grow out of her . . ." Carol's voice faded away as she gazed over to the other side of the canteen. "Look at her now. Snotty little bitch."

The Porters and the Kerridges were next-door neighbors on Jubilee Terrace, and (barring occasional upsets) bosom friends. They were fixtures for as long as the powers-that-be would allow them to be on Britain's most popular soap. The Porters had had just the one son, a ne'er-do-well youth who had emigrated to Australia, where he was said, as even Mr. Micawber was said, to be doing well. The Kerridges had a son and a daughter. The son was in the Merchant Navy. The actor who wants out of a soap is usually either killed or sent to the colonies. If he wants out with the option of occasional return spots he is as often as not sent to sea with the Royal or Merchant Navy. The fact that Britain hardly has a fleet of any kind these days has not impinged on the world of soaps. The next the great British public hears of him is likely to be at Christmas, when he stars in pantomime, that most degraded of musical fairy stories for children.

Which left the Kerridges' daughter. Dawn was her soap name, and ten years back she had been an enchanting child—played by a dire little tot from stage school, now with the Royal Shakespeare Company and infinitely contemptuous of television soaps. Dawn had disappeared from the series for a time, spoken of but not seen, and she had reappeared four years before, a pretty, pouting sixteen, and played by Susan Fyldes.

The two women stared over to where Susan was deep in conversation with Dawn's current boyfriend, a young black actor with a pronounced public school accent.

"I wouldn't mind," said Carol, in a boding-ill voice, "if she didn't keep throwing it at you how bloody wellborn she is."

"Oh yes, we've all been told her family limps back to the seventeenth century," agreed Marjorie. "Who cares? And it's hard to see that as a qualification for working on *Jubilee Terrace*."

"But she's a good little actress," said Carol, very obviously trying to be fair. "She's got the accent off almost as well as you have, and she does the sweet ingenue to the life."

"But a shade vacuous, don't you feel?"

"Well, but that's not a drawback. The Kerridges in general are hardly likely to produce a mastermind."

"There is a blankness behind the eyes—the ultimate giveaway," pronounced Marjorie magisterially. "Look at early Elizabeth Taylor films." She watched the young pair's close, conversing heads. "She seems to be getting on better with James at the moment."

"Darling, she *detests* him. It's just as with you and Vernon. They're good professionals."

"He's certainly wonderfully handsome," said Marjorie. "I could fancy him myself."

"Fancy, yes," agreed Carol. "But not *like*. Considering that the two of them are currently the nation's sweethearts they are neither of them very high in the likeability stakes."

"I know Bill absolutely loathes James," said Marjorie. "He's been like a bear with a sore head ever since James came into the series. Look at him now—just *gazing* at them."

They looked toward another table, where Bill Garrett and his *Jubilee Terrace* wife, Liza Croome, were drinking halves of lager. Bill and Liza played Bob and Sally Worseley, licensees of the Duke of York's. The character of Bob, established as the pub landlord since the series began, was an ex-boxer, now publican, whose barmaid wife was a perpetual source of anxiety and sexual jealousy. Rather unfortunately, life mirrored fiction, for Bill was in fact an ex-boxer whose tarty wife at home, and her goings-on with all and sundry, had provided staple canteen gossip for the *Terrace* cast since time immemorial. The fact that the wife had an occasional role in the *Terrace* did not help matters. Liza Croome, however, was the reverse of her television role: her blowsiness was a matter of makeup and accent, and she was in reality a gentle and warmhearted soul who had acted as shoulder-to-weep-on to Bill in his emotional troubles more often than she cared to remember.

"Of course Bill's dislike of James is *racial*," said Marjorie, with that air of omniscience that many found irritating. "We all dislike James, but Bill dislikes him because he is black."

"How do you make that out?" asked Carol. "I've never heard him use racial epithets, not about James or anyone else—and he would if that was the way he thought. Bill is rather uncouth underneath."

"He's rather uncouth on top. But it's obvious. Bill was a boxer. All the best boxers are black. He must have been knocked to the canvas—is that the expression?—countless times by black boxers, because he was never very *good*. I'm sure he nurses a grudge."

"You're going off into one of your fantasy worlds," said Carol. "Bill was never a boxer, except to get a bit of money while he put himself through drama school. We all did the same—waitressing, barmaiding, right down to going on the game. Bill doesn't nurse grudges through half a lifetime, and certainly not about being knocked to the canvas." She leaned forward. "But I think there is a quite different explanation."

"And what is that?"

"I think Bill fancies Susan."

"But he's old enough to be her father!"

"Didn't we just agree we fancied James?"

Liza Croome sat beside Bill Garrett in what once would have been companionable silence. They had often been thus—or else Bill had sat there, telling her in a low voice and hopeless tones about the latest exploits of his wife. They were exceptionally close, though there was not a spark of sexual attraction between them. Liza knew him through and through, liked being near him, and could predict his every reaction. Almost as if I *were* his wife, she often thought—the wife in a long-established marriage that had settled into a comfortable and comforting routine.

But in the last few weeks a new element had entered their relationship, something she did not quite know how to cope with.

"*Bill,*" she said, a clear note of warning in her voice.

Bill sat up and shook himself.

"Sorry, I was miles away."

"What were you thinking about?" she asked, her voice back into neutral.

He turned to her, squared his shoulders, and said, as if he had received a sudden, divine clarification, "I've decided to leave Bet."

It was what Liza had been urging him to do for years. Bet was no good for him—no good for anyone. She was a whore with a heart of steel. Now it had come, and Liza felt the need to inject a note of caution.

"I'm glad. But it won't do any good, you know."

"What do you mean?"

Liza nodded toward the table where Susan and James sat, still close and absorbed.

"The only thing that will do any good there is to keep out of Susan's way as much as possible—go out to the pub when she comes to the canteen, keep away from her dressing room, keep away from her on set. Just don't go near her."

"Come off it. You don't think I have hopes—"

"You have dreams, which is no better. You let them invade real life, and that's dangerous. You've just got to close down on the whole thing—like any other fire."

Bill Garrett looked away from her.

"She's of age to come into the pub in a fortnight's time," he muttered.

"What do you mean? Susan's twenty. She's been going to pubs for years."

"Not Susan, Dawn Kerridge. Dawn, the character, will be of age to come into the Duke of York's. There'll be a lot more scenes involving the two of us."

That was true, and unwelcome. Liza Croome wished that Susan would find a steady boyfriend, though she rather thought that at the moment she too much relished her position as sexual tease to the male cast of *Jubilee Terrace* and to the males of the nation at large.

"We'll insist on a close-up of the two of us there," said James. "When you say, 'I've never done it seriously before. Only at school for fun.'"

"That's right. And they can hold it for 'I thought I was

serious, but it was never like this.' Christ, what an awful line!"

"Ghastly. But pure soap. It would be a pity to change it. Then they can back off a bit for the next lines, and then come closer as our two faces come together for the kiss, and you go down onto the bed."

"Cut. Cut before I get there. Reggie will insist on that. Leaving the mugs in doubt whether we do or we don't."

"And in fact we *don't,* because that's going to come up in about six weeks' time. Will we, won't we? God, what a sickening pair. A pantomime would be a greater challenge." James stood up. "Right. That's all settled. I don't think Reggie will disagree about the close-ups. See you on set."

He nodded brusquely and walked away. As she watched his back, Susan thought: I could go for him, if he wasn't such a shit.

And, walking away, James Selcott—Will Brown in the soap—thought the equivalent. He generally referred to her to outsiders as a pricktease with pretensions. Their judgments, in both cases, were eminently fair.

Lady Wharton sat in a corner of the main set, learning her lines. Winnie Hey, who played her, found remembering anything increasingly difficult as she got older. Winnie loved sitting on the *Terrace* set, felt that it was as good as sitting in the garden. The houses were small, though room by room each had been enlarged over the years. The scriptwriters wished they had made them larger than the traditional two up, two down. Then extra characters could be moved in and out more convincingly. As it was, one house could contain six or seven characters without it being explained where they all slept. The scriptwriters relied on viewers not noticing, but a regular trickle of mail testified to the fact that the devoted viewer did. A two-bedroom house containing three generations of a family, with boyfriends or girlfriends in and out, was obviously full to bursting.

Lady Wharton had been a brainwave of Reggie Friedman, the director, about five years before. Not one of the other soaps, he insisted, had a member of the aristocracy in it. Why should the aristocracy be discriminated against? It could prove a trump card: *Jubilee Terrace* would be the only British soap with snob appeal. He carried the day: the people responsible for soaps love "onlys" and "firsts." Cyril Wharton had moved into a flat in the Terrace as the advance guard. He was a stage designer, and it was made clear that he was excessively mothered, and escaping from apron strings. His sexual leanings were sketched in, but they almost never met with success with the sturdy working-class boys of the Terrace. Cyril decorated the spacious ground-floor flat as if it were a set for *Lady Windermere's Fan*. Not long after that his mother had moved in, and not long after that Cyril had fled to the more welcoming environment of San Francisco.

But Lady Wharton had remained in Jubilee Terrace. It was never quite explained why, but it was delicately hinted that she was genteelly hard up. Her elder son, the present baronet, was something of a brute in merchant banking. Anyway, there she was, the Terrace's cut-price

Lady Bracknell—cut-price only because the posse of scriptwriters never thought up lines for her anything like as good as Wilde's. Winnie was overjoyed she had been kept in the show. Stable employment was something to be valued at her age. She had been hard up all her life—and not genteelly so. At times she had been cold, she had been hungry. Now she had recognition on buses and tubes, and above all butter on her bread. It was something a young actor might throw away, but not an old one. It was worth clinging to. Winnie, frowning, concentrated on her lines.

"The haddock you sold me yesterday was so dubious even the cat thought twice," she intoned.

"Hello, Winnie."

It was Reggie Friedman, breezing by. He was always breezing by, or throwing information at you in rapid staccato and not waiting for your reaction. Reggie had been the principal director of *Jubilee Terrace* for seven years, and still seemed to revel in it. This time, for once, he darted over.

"I've had a marvelous idea, Winnie. To fill the gap left by Bert Porter's death. I thought of bringing back the Kerridge boy, but Ian has got a long-term contract with the Glasgow Citizens, and he's not interested till next year at the earliest. But I've come up with something much better. We'll have Cyril back."

Winnie's voice suddenly failed her. By the time she did get out, "Oh no, not Cyril," Reggie was in the full flood of enthusiasm.

"Yes. Isn't it a great idea? Back from San Francisco. Big mystery. Why has he come home? And you know why? He's got tuberculosis. Come home to die. Isn't that a fabulous plotline? None of the other soaps has woken up to the resurgence of tuberculosis. We've all had tactful looks at senile dementia. And of course there isn't a soap that hasn't done AIDS. But all the time TB has been staging a comeback."

"Is tuberculosis rife in San Francisco?" Winnie asked faintly. But Reggie was edging away.

"Who cares? We'll have got in first. It's a plotline to die for, and a real trailblazer."

To his departing back Winnie Hey wailed, "Not Cyril. Please, Reggie. Not Hamish Fawley."

But by then Reggie had disappeared through the swing doors. It was some time before Winnie thought of a crumb of comfort: if tuberculosis was to be the story line that brought Cyril back, it was likely that his reappearance would be terminal.

Bill Garrett had phoned his wife, Bet, from the car, so when he arrived home she already had her coat on and they did no more than pass in the doorway.

"Angela's out, Debbie and Rosie are in their rooms. You can fucking babysit—I've had them all day."

"They're not babies, and they've been at school most of the day. Where are you going?"

"What do you care? Anyway, you're not my fucking probation officer."

And she breezed out.

Bill went to the kitchen and made himself a cup of tea. Upstairs he heard his two younger daughters shouting between bedrooms. They always gave him a bit of time when he got home—time to stop being pub-keeper Bob Worseley and to start being Bill again was how they put it—and he appreciated their consideration. They were lovely girls, all three of them, the center of his life. It was as if nothing of their mother had gone into their making. They were kind, concerned, intelligent—none of those words you could apply to Bet.

Sipping his tea, Bill considered his resolution to divorce his wife. Certainly she had given him more than enough reason, and she gave him almost daily evidence that she only stayed with him for materialistic reasons—food, drink, heating, lighting, pocket money, and a degree of local cachet as the wife of a television personality.

There was, in fact, nothing left of the marriage, not for her and certainly not for him. He had no doubt she would prefer him to have custody of the children. Why had he not cut the knot years ago? He could only assume it was the pull of habit, a fear of having full responsibility for the girls. But that wasn't something he feared—more something he desired. He would protect them from the contamination of contact with their mother. He concluded it was his habitual lethargy that held him back, just as it had held him back from quitting *Jubilee Terrace* and entering the unknown, terrifying world of being a jobbing actor, one with no clear idea of where the next job, and the next check, were going to come from. He had been guilty of lethargy—lethargy and cowardice. Well, no longer.

"Daddy," said Rosie, as she and Debbie and the returned Angela (nine, twelve, and fifteen) sat on or around him on the sofa half an hour later. "Did Mummy tell you?"

"I shouldn't think so," said Bill. "We didn't have time for many words."

"She's going back into *Jubilee Terrace*. Three weeks' work."

"They might have informed me. When's this?"

"Early next month."

"So soon. Why didn't they let her know earlier?"

"I don't know. She seemed pleased."

I bet she seemed pleased, said Bill to himself. Bet loved her occasional sorties into the *Terrace*. They were a heaven-sent opportunity to humiliate him. Who would her object of attention be this time? Reggie? James? No, not the latter. Bill couldn't see the suave young man courting sneers by going with a brassy woman of forty-two. Maybe the returned Hamish, who was in real life as hetero as the character he played was not.

One thing was for certain: Bet would be out to humiliate him, but now he would be just as determined to humiliate her. He remembered, back in the days when *EastEnders* was watchable, Dirty Den serving divorce papers on Angie as her much-trumpeted Christmas present. Pity Christmas was so far in the future. Halloween would hardly have the same effect. Even Easter would have been something. Still, he could make the divorce decision as public as possible.

Then he sighed.

He wasn't that sort of man. Not loud, not public, not demonstrative. He'd do things privately, softly, considerately. He wondered in his mind whether Bet had ever done anything considerately in her life. Never, he thought. Never.

CHAPTER 2

A Wedding

✳

The vicar who married Arthur Bradley and Maureen Cooke was drunk.

"Will you shake this woman—?" he asked, his voice wet with spittle.

Arthur and Maureen stood there, he uncomfortable in his best suit, she in a white dress she was scarcely entitled to, and both looking miserable and embarrassed.

"Will you take this woman," the vicar tried again, "to be your awful wedded wife. Hey! Thatsh Dylan Thomash. I was in that play once."

"Cut!" shouted Reggie Friedman. He marched up to the vicar in one of his great rages. "You . . . are . . . drunk."

"Sho what? The vicar of St. Jude's has an alcohol problem. Wouldn't be the firsht time in the Shurch of England."

Reggie, getting pinker by the moment, poked his finger into the vicar's surplice.

"The vicar of St. Jude's does not have an alcohol problem. *You* have an alcohol problem. Or, to put it more plainly, you have become a congenital drunk. You have also become a liability to *Jubilee Terrace*. Go away and put your head under the cold tap, and come back in five minutes. If you can't get it right then, you're *out*, Get me? OUT! Location filming costs money, and I'm not going to waste any more of it on your imbecilities."

Reggie strode back down the aisle of St. Peter's, Northwick, the Victorian Gothic edifice that always stood in as St. Jude's, the *Jubilee Terrace* parish church, on such occasions. He was livid. George Price had once been a reliable small-part actor. Now he was a lush. He felt the sleeve of his jacket being pulled, and he looked down to see Gladys Porter, in the shape of Marjorie Harcourt-Smith.

"You can't really mean that you'd sack George," she said, too shortsighted to see the implacable expression on Reggie's face. "He's always been the St. Jude's vicar. He married the Kerridge boy, did Dawn's confirmation, and buried—"

"Spare me the hatches, matches, and dispatches, Marjorie."

"But you wouldn't sack him, would you, Reggie? So publicly? He's *always* been the *Jubilee Terrace* vicar."

"So you keep saying. But actually it's only been for the last five years. I gave him the part, and I've had my eye on him, believe you me. He's made most of the funerals almost jolly. So unless he comes back sober, this is the last sacrament of holy matrimony he will conduct in this church."

Marjorie and Carol Chisholm, sitting together, looked

shocked at Reggie's relish. He could have been a malignant Archbishop of Canterbury.

"But how will you explain his being replaced?"

"Crisis of faith? Gone to a retreat? Gone into rehab?" He straightened and regarded the congregation—Winnie Hey in the row behind; Bet Garrett, just slipping in through the front door; Susan and James, sitting together but separate; Liza Croome looking concerned but understanding. Then he swiveled around to see the happy couple, with Bill Garrett being best man before the altar. He muttered to Marjorie in a very distinct and determined mutter, "Back in my office filing cabinet I've got a hundred reasons for writing new characters in and a thousand for writing old characters out, either temporarily or permanently. *None* of you is indispensable. Got it?"

Oh, they had got it. At heart they had always known it. And in fact it was in its way a comfort, especially for the younger actors: should that call come from the National Theatre, should that Hollywood film materialize, they would not be letting the side down by accepting. The show would go on.

The show, at present, was a wedding that could have taken place at any time over the past three or four years. Arthur Bradley had come to *Jubilee Terrace* as a bluff, slightly randy art teacher. Then, with the versatility that characterizes soap opera destinies, he had taken over the corner shop. Maureen Cooke was at the time in the throes of marital difficulties that had viewers ringing and writing in with advice and support. After her divorce it was not long before she took up with Arthur, and soon she was moving in with him, taking her children, and helping to run the shop. By now she also had a baby by him. Whether the Bradleys should have been, or could have been, married in church was a point that did not bother the writers of *Jubilee Terrace*. They were being married now so that the event could joyfully offset the death of Bert Porter. A Registry Office wedding wouldn't have fitted the bill at all.

Now Garry Kopps and Shirley Merritt (who played Arthur and Maureen) were standing at the altar feeling rather foolish. This seemed like a very ceremonial form of coitus interruptus. Bill Garrett, holding the ring as if it were a hot potato, looked equally disconcerted, but his unease was due to the sudden appearance of his wife. She was not a good argument for weddings in any of their forms. Reggie Friedman had gone to the back of the church, where a finishing class from the West Yorkshire College of Music and Drama was watching filming. Reggie was eyeing them speculatively. The congregation, meanwhile, was talking in low tones, as congregations will do in real life. The fact of being in church was affecting the actors.

"I think it'll be an awful shame if Reggie does replace the vicar," said Winnie Hey, Lady Wharton, leaning forward to talk to Marjorie Harcourt-Smith in almost inaudible tones. "The vicar and the doctor are not exactly characters, but they're both what you might call *touch-stones* in *Jubilee Terrace*."

"A drunken vicar is no sort of touchstone," said Marjorie reasonably. "Now I've thought it over, I see Reggie's point. He has no choice. If he filmed him in his present

state he'd get protests from Alcohol Concern, and probably from the Church of England high-ups as well."

"I hate to see the old characters go," said Carol
Chisholm.

"I hate to see some of them come back," said Winnie.
"Hamish Fawley being a case in point. But not the old
dependables who represent the community at large."

"I suppose a drunk vicar could represent the community," said Marjorie thoughtfully. "Characters in soaps
seem to spend even more time drinking than they do
sleeping around."

Winnie Hey nodded, taking the point seriously.

"I love this sort of session," she said contentedly.
"When you get paid just for sitting around and being
seen, and having hardly any lines."

"You'll be getting your share of the action when your
Cyril comes back," said Carol. Winnie shuddered.

"Don't mention Cyril's Second Coming," she said. "I
did go to the scriptwriters and put it to them that the
treatment should be mainly Hamish lying in bed looking
pale and interesting, and me sitting by it looking
anguished. Even that would have taxed my acting abili-
ties, because a wasting disease is what Hamish has been
asking for for years. My God, what a *toad* that man is!
Anyway, they weren't having any. They said it would be
an inadequate representation of the *Jubilee Terrace*
response to the renewed threat of TB."

"What did they mean by that?"

"I don't imagine even they knew. But what was clear is
that there are going to be a lot of confrontations between

him and other characters, and lots of dramatic scenes between him and me. Sheer hell—and millions of lines to learn."

James Selcott and Susan Fyldes—as Will and Dawn, much written about and photographed in *Hello, Hi!*, and *Girlie Talk* magazines—sat toward the back, slumped in their pew, their faces a mingling of boredom, melancholy, and contempt. It was in just such a mood that James, in reply to the inevitable question from a *Hi!* reporter as to whether there was anything between him and Susan, had replied, "I can have any chick I want at the click of my fingers. Why should I settle for one?" He had been not just ungrateful when *Hi!* tactfully suppressed the quote but convulsed with rage.

"I *loathe* this sort of scene," said James, deciding that talking was the lesser of two evils. "Nothing to do, no point to make—not even the usual dim, soap opera kind of point."

"I think," said the coy voice of an extra from the pew behind, "that you're both meant to be sitting there wondering whether it will be your turn next."

"I'd rather die," said James and Susan simultaneously.

Suddenly the congregation was hushed. The vicar had returned. He was not walking straight, neither was he looking penitent. And he could be smelled from the tenth row. Whatever he had put his head under, it had not been water.

"Dearly beloved," he yelled cheerily, producing a bottle from under his surplice, "we are tethered together—"

"Right!" said Reggie Friedman, marching forward.

"That's it! That's the end! You're defrocked, or unsmocked, or whatever the damned word is. You're fired!"

"You can't fire me," said the vicar, weaving joyously backward to gain support from the altar. "How are you going to get this fucking pair married?"

"They'll get married if I have to do it myself." Reggie turned to two stalwart props men. "Get him out of here, get that bloody surplice off him, and boot him out of the church. And dig out some air fresheners. The place smells like a distillery. We'll be lucky if we don't have to pay to have it reconsecrated."

Without waiting to see whether his orders were obeyed (rather as Queen Victoria sat down without looking to see whether the chair was there, knowing it would be), Reggie strode down the aisle to the gaggle of drama students at the back of the church.

"Right. How many of you have got Equity cards?"

A straggling six or seven put up their hands, expressions of pathetic eagerness on their faces.

"Men—it's got to be a man."

"No, it doesn't," said an eager girl. "Women can conduct marriage services or do anything else you can name in the C of E these days."

"Not in *Jubilee Terrace* they can't . . . Let's see . . . *You*." Reggie pointed to a gangling youth, a bean-pole six-foot body topped by a cherubic face. "Let's hear your voice."

"Dearly beloved, we are gathered here today in the sight of God—"

"What's your name?"

"Stephen Barrymore."

Robert Barnard

"Good man. Might be lucky. Now, you're on. Go to Makeup in the vestry, then get the surplice on. It'll be too short, but we'll make do with close-ups of head and shoulders. And we'll call you . . . let's think . . . Kevin Plunkett. Right?"

It was a fairy tale transformation, the British equivalent of the waitress at the Hollywood soda fountain. Stephen Barrymore would get national coverage in a top-of-the-viewing-figures episode of *Terrace*. The other students' faces showed a mixture of wonder, delight, and biliousness.

Reggie, in the wait, improvised like the professional he was. He walked up the aisle, looking around him speculatively. He picked Lady Wharton and the Kerridges, and sat down on his haunches in the aisle beside them, summoning cameras and sound equipment in a lordly manner with his hands.

"Something to paper over the change," he said. "Why isn't the usual vicar doing the service? What's the best line? Has he gone into a retreat?"

"Hospital would be better," said Philip Marston, who played Peter Kerridge. "People don't always come out of hospital."

"Right. Good thinking. Here's what you say . . ."

And so it was filmed. Lady Wharton leaned over to the Kerridges and whispered, "It's the new curate. While the vicar is in hospital."

"What's wrong with him?" asked Norma Kerridge.

"I don't know. But his family are looking very worried."

And so the way was paved for George Price's departure from the serial. A drunken star might perforce be tolerated, had been often enough in this and other soaps, but a drunken bit-part player was as expendable as a spent match.

Particularly as the new curate looked and spoke the part to perfection.

"Will you, Arthur Bradley," he piped, in a voice that seemed to have broken only yesterday, with a benign smile that suggested he had no notion they had been sleeping together for years, "take this woman, Maureen Cooke . . ."

The pair stood there, half-proud, half-sheepish, making their responses firmly. The congregation buzzed with satisfaction. It was going to be a lovely wedding. Bet Garrett, Bill's wife, who played Rita Somerville, a florist with a fine line in snobbery and spite, whispered cynically to her neighbor, "Bill's enjoying this, the bastard. All we had was a measly Registry Office affair."

"That'd be all Arthur and Maureen would have had," said the neighbor, "in real life."

"Oh, don't talk about real life. In real life Bill's a lousy husband, but he's obviously going to be a pillar of strength to Maureen, Arthur, and the kids. It ought to be as unlucky to mention real life on a soap set as to say *Macbeth* in the theater . . ."

The ring bit went well, with Bill, as Bob Worseley the best man, making a nice thing out of forgetting which pocket it was in. Actually he *had* forgotten which pocket he had it in. Maureen squeezed some genuine tears as they were made man and wife, and the cameras caught their glisten. Garry Kopps as Arthur looked proud and pleased as punch as he and his new wife walked down the aisle, and there was a jolly little scene as they signed the book.

"Do you know that was my first wedding?" the new curate improvised, as he shook their hands and wished them well.

"I couldn't have done it better myself," said Arthur.

Reggie was delighted, and said he'd keep it in. He took the new curate's address for Accounts and Casting, and said that—who knew?—there might be something else for him before too long.

"We've got a TB sequence coming soon. You know—young man dying. The curate could play a part."

"Strike a blow against the 'brought here from the Indian subcontinent' school of thought?" asked Stephen Barrymore sagely.

"Right. That could be effective. Start a lot of discussion, which is what we like. With all these programs where the viewer talks back, discussion is of the essence, though, God knows, ninety-five percent of it is unutterable tripe. Well, as I say, we may be in touch . . . Kevin Plunkett the curate. Nice sound, eh?"

Outside the police had thrown a cordon around the spectators, the real spectators, come to see the cast of *Jubilee Terrace.* They were kept well back, while the mock spectators—the congregation at the wedding of Arthur and Maureen—gathered on the steps of the church, little bags of confetti in their hands. Reggie Friedman was in an ecstasy of busyness arranging the cast and the extras in the best positions.

"I'm going to do it once," he said, "just the once.

They're going to come out, and your reactions will be what's shown. So get it right."

It was in the final moments before Arthur and Maureen came through the door that a youngish man approached one of the policemen keeping back the knot of real spectators. Luckily the constable had been a viewer before he joined the force (there had been precious little time since), and he recognized the man and let him through. The man strolled down the street, smiling an inward, brooding smile, as the cheers were rehearsed and as, eventually, the happy couple emerged through the church door. The cheers were joyous, the confetti hit its target, and the couple walked through the church gate to the waiting limousine.

The man approached the gate, where Bet Garrett was watching the regulars in the cast. She and the man stood for a moment together.

"Hi, Terracers, I'm back," he shouted.

It was well that the scene of jubilation was in the can.

"*Bloody* Hamish," hissed Winnie Hey, and next to her, she could feel Bill Garrett's body stiffen at the sight of Bet. The St. Jude's congregation stared at the young man, stoney-faced.

Only Reggie Friedman, smiling and enthusiastic, ran down the church steps to greet him.

"Hamish!" he said. "Welcome home!"

CHAPTER 3

In Sickness
and in Health

The face on the bed was fearsomely white. Hamish Fawley had never played Cyril as one of television's perma-
tanned homosexuals, but this was extreme. It was the
makeup department's way of saying to the viewers: this is
serious, my friends. This may not be a deathbed, but it
sure as hell is going to lead to one.

Winnie Hey was flustered. She had read her scripts in
the chronological order of her scenes, and had forgotten
to check the order of their filming. If she had, she would
have realized that Cyril's first bout of serious illness after
his homecoming was to be filmed before the homecoming
itself, at Leeds/Bradford airport. She was word-perfect, or
as near as she ever got, for the airport sequence, but a
long way from it for the bedroom scene.

"Mother," croaked Cyril, in an interestingly attenu-
ated voice, "there's something I haven't told you."

"I'm sure there are *many* things you haven't told me,"
the old lady said grimly.

"No, but this is . . . different. The fact is, I've got tuberculosis."

There was a long silence. Eventually the pathetically dying face twisted into a snarl.

"Oh, for God's sake, you stupid old cow. You've forgotten your lines again. Why do I have to have all my big scenes with someone in the Alzheimer's zone?"

"I haven't forgotten my lines," protested Winnie. "Lady Wharton's flabbergasted by the news. Naturally. She thought tuberculosis was something in the past. She doesn't know how to react."

"Doesn't know how to react? Why—does she think tuberculosis is a garden flower?"

"There's no pause in the script, Winnie," said Reggie Friedman. "If you put one in as long as you have done it'll only be cut out. Your next line is 'But nobody gets tuberculosis these days.'"

"Of course it is. I knew that," said Winnie unconvincingly. "Let's go back to Cyril's last line."

"Oh, for God's sake," muttered Cyril. He laid his head back on the pillow, assumed a faraway expression, and brought back the distant tones of visiting royalty. "But this is different, Mother. The fact is, I've got tuberculosis."

Winnie left a small pause to make a point, then said, "Tuberculosis? But nobody gets tuberculosis these days."

She did it rather well, managing to get incredulity and fear into her voice.

"Oh, but they do, Mumsie. It's been hibernating, biding its time. And now it's come back, with a vengeance."

"But there must be drugs these days, things to cure it."

"You'd think so, wouldn't you? But not always. There

27

are things that sometimes work, or slow things down. I've tried all of them."

There was another long pause.

"Oh, for God's sake!" came again from the bed.

"Look, Winnie," said Reggie, "here's the script. Read the lines, and we'll film you from behind."

"Why don't you just film her ankles," said Hamish. "She says they used to be her best feature a century or so ago. They're probably the only part of her that can act."

"Just get the words approximately right," said Reggie encouragingly. "Say something appropriate to the situation."

"I'm finding it difficult to find words that express anything except my delight at Cyril's approaching death," said Winnie.

It was Garry Kopps and Shirley Merritt's first day back on the *Jubilee Terrace* sets after their "marriage." They had been granted a rather lavish four weeks' break, approximating a honeymoon, which according to the script had been spent in the Bahamas. Now they were back, and Shirley had to be made up differently, to hide the fact that she had spent the four free weeks not on the beach but at home in York.

Once they'd filmed Arthur and Maureen's arrival back at the corner shop their time was free until four, so the two actors did what they often did—took sandwiches and a couple of cans of beer out to one of the Leeds parks. This time they went to Kirkstall, and sat on the medieval masonry in weather that was ridiculously warm for October. Garry was meditating writing a cozy and personal book on his time on *Jubilee Terrace* and another on soaps in general, their codes and their limitations as social documents. Garry was the intellectual of the cast.

"So what's gone on while I've been away?" he asked.

"Hmmm. I haven't been hanging around the studio, so I may have missed all sorts of things."

"Come off it. Someone will have been on the phone to you with all the important stuff. And failing that, you'd have phoned someone and pried it out of them."

"Well, I just do it for you, Garry. I'm only interested in my painting. Let's see: Hamish's return you saw yourself. All that followed it was entirely predictable: he spread his usual bile and contempt for all and every one of us, mainly for Winnie."

"I suppose you talked to her. How's she taking it?"

"She's upset, of course, but comforting herself that there will soon be an end to Cyril without it entailing an end for her. The trouble is that all the emotional disturbance means she finds it still more difficult to concentrate on her lines. She's beginning to improvise on her scripts, which gives Hamish more ammunition."

"I frankly don't see Hamish having many good scenes before he snuffs it. In the nature of things there aren't many likely situations he can be put into."

"Reggie is thinking of bringing back the curate."

"The one in the church? The student? A bit untried, isn't he? An unknown quantity."

"He struck me as a lovely lad."

"No," said Garry, with all the pedantry of an academic sociologist. "He played the part of a lovely lad very convincingly. You love confusing real life with unreal life."

"Oh well, I bet he'll fit in beautifully. There's already a debate started on whether he could get Cyril to pray with him on his deathbed."

"Good God! That's a bit different from our usual debates about whether X should sleep with Y, or whether Z should give up smoking."

"It's the fact that it's a bit different that's making people want it. If it's done, it'll be done very tactfully. No chorus of welcoming angels heralding Cyril's entry to heaven. Nothing Gounod-ish."

"OK—what else?"

"Hamish has taken a strong dislike to Susan and James."

"Tell me something surprising. I'd have thought he'd have taken against Susan ages ago. James is too recent."

"Hamish and Susan hardly had any scenes together during his first spell on the *Terrace*. He was usually in the pub with his mother, Susan as the teenager usually in the family home. Now he finds the romance between her and James saccharine (as we all do) and horribly politically correct. Most people think he's just jealous of James's good looks."

"What form has the bile taken?"

"One thing Marjorie quoted to me was: 'These days young dimwits go to drama school because they can't get an apprenticeship in plumbing.'"

"Charming. As opposed to those young ladies in our day who went to drama school as a cheaper alternative to finishing school in Switzerland."

"They still do, actually. And can you just see James as a plumber?"

"Never in a million years. That's one of the interesting

things about Hamish. His bile comes out with tremendous venom, but it is nearly always misdirected, remote from the truth. It's like scattershot: only one in fifty missiles hits its target."

"Anyway, the truth is that the atmosphere on the set has deteriorated significantly."

"What was Reggie thinking of, bringing Hamish back?"

"Bill Garrett asked Reggie that. He said a fiery atmosphere keeps everyone on their toes. Too much sweetness and light and all the viewers sense is lethargy."

"Ho-ho! I think he doth protest too much."

"What do you mean by that?"

"I mean there must have been some other reason—at present not known—for bringing Hamish back. Watch this space."

"Reggie is almost the only one around who's speaking to Hamish. That niggles our Hamish. He needs someone to make his vicious remarks to. That remark about apprentice plumbers was made in the canteen to Reggie. He should have protested and put him in his place, but he only made his excuses and left."

"Coward. Ah, well, you could say it's business as usual."

"No. Marjorie says it's *much* worse than usual."

"People romanticize the past when they're thinking about the present. I must say, when I first heard of the death of Vernon Watts I assumed someone had pushed him under that bus."

"All of us felt the desire to, at one time or another."

"Well, if anyone took action, they've got away with it nicely."

The name of Vernon Watts came up in the *Jubilee Terrace* studio that same day. Filming was "outside" in the Terrace itself, and there were plenty of places on the much-used permanent set to sit around and gossip.

"Oh, I do miss Vernon," sighed Marjorie to Philip Marston, Carol's soap husband.

"Someone familiar you know through and through?"

"Something like that. Someone whose reactions I know through and through, is perhaps closer. Someone who I could have a really convincing row with, even someone I could, at a pinch, enjoy making up with."

"Sounds like real-life matrimony," said Philip.

"Well, it *was* in many ways. A love-hate affair. The love part just means it's someone you *know*, are totally familiar with."

"I suppose that's the truth about Bill and Bet."

"I think the love there is even feebler than Vernon's and mine."

"Anyway, there's Melvin. Visiting us toilers at the coal face. Why don't you have a word with him?" And he gestured to the man wearing the cravat and velvet jacket, which suggested that he was essentially, or at least wanted to be thought, an artistic gentleman of a bygone era.

Melvin's official title was head of scripts. There was in fact a legion of writers for the five-times-a-week soap, but Melvin was keeper of the flame, the one who had absolute power of sanction or veto on all plot developments and even over casual fill-in material. He was, as far as anybody knew, a happily married man who had a family in Ilkley but who, at work, had a power nearly absolute, especially as he and Reggie tended to be of one mind. Melvin liked his power. "Your life or your death are in my hands," he would say; "you are just the putty, for me to make with what I like." Sometimes cast members begged him to kill them off, to make for them the decision that, because of family commitments, they were not strong enough to make for themselves. But most of the cast regarded Melvin with a sort of affectionate fear.

"So what is occupying the minds of you dear people?" he inquired (even his vocabulary was a thing of the past).

"It's Marjorie," said Philip. "She needs a new somebody in her life."

"Ah—the usual thing," said Melvin, instantly sympathetic. "You didn't expect to, but you miss Vernon."

"Yes, I do," admitted Marjorie. "All those rows we had, but at least he was somebody who could be—well, a sort of sounding board. Now Gladys Porter has nobody in her life like that—nobody of first-rate importance to her. Do you get my meaning?"

"Oh, absolutely. Everybody who suffers loss feels the same, whether it's soap loss or real-life loss. If we'd just written Vernon out you wouldn't be feeling so very different. He wouldn't have been around for you anymore. It's perfectly natural."

"The question is, what are you going to do about it?" said Philip.

Melvin thought.

"Well, I don't have to do anything, you know. New widows don't find that God immediately provides them with a new significant other. He just lets the bereaved one jog on in loneliness as often as not."

"But *you* could put someone into my life—a love or a hate—to give meaning to what I do," said Marjorie in a wheedling voice.

"Oh yes—I'm far nicer than God in many respects. I will think it over, bring it up at Thursday's script conference." He was starting away when his eye was caught by the set of the Terrace. From the house that was Lady Wharton and Cyril's home Hamish Fawley had emerged, white-faced, stepping mincingly across the cobbles, triumphantly resurrecting the walk that had been discarded by homosexuals two decades before. Melvin turned to the other two.

"You know, when you called me over I thought you were going to protest about Hamish's return. Why didn't you? Everyone else has."

"We knew they would have," said Philip. "So why bother? We do like to be a bit original, Marjorie and I. But what possessed Reggie to bring Hamish back?"

"He fills the gap left by Vernon. As you know, Marjorie, you and Vernon were to have had a strong story line about now. Cyril is the substitute, as to a lesser degree Bet Garrett is too. Both are stopgaps, of course."

"Thank God for that," said Philip.

"Well, all I can say is, you owe me a good story line," said Marjorie.

"Point taken." Melvin paused again in his exit. "You know, I once knew someone quite as horrible as Hamish . . . many years ago, when I was a young man, thinking to write the Great Novel. He was utterly contemptuous of all moral codes, kicked over all the usual restraints that people observe, made clear he loved hurting people, watching them flinch . . . He was just a bundle of putrefaction."

"Who was he? What did he do?"

"Actually he was a pimp. With a train of suffering women anxious to break free of him but not able to. I disliked the sex trade then, and I still do. We've never had a prostitute in *Jubilee Terrace*."

"Name me a soap that has had a prostitute in it," said Philip.

"*Coronation Street*'s had an 'escort,'" said Melvin thoughtfully. "But a common-or-garden prostitute—no . . . Interesting."

Hamish Fawley as Cyril Wharton tiptoed into the newsagency, each exaggerated step becoming teensy-weensier the closer he got to the camera. The presentation of Cyril in *Jubilee Terrace* was to be double-headed, after initial consultations among Hamish, Melvin, and Reggie. With his intimate friends—notably his mother and the Kerridges—he was a man like any other, straightforward, opinionated, natural. With the Terrace in general, the solidly working-class characters, he became the stereotypical homosexual of popular myth, the camp queen of radio and television humor now decades out of date. His characterization was intended as an emetic, to ridicule prejudice and buried fear. In the present scene he was regarded with distaste by Harry Hornby, the newsagent—a distaste dictated by the character's homophobia but also simply the actor's reaction to Hamish himself.

"The *Guardian*, is it?" Hornby asked, putting his voice into neutral.

"Oh yes. One must keep up, mustn't one, for as long as one can." Cyril looked around the little shop. "And there is something else—but it's rather embarrassing."

"Oh?"

"I'm that most pathetic creature—a man so short he can't reach up to the top shelf in a newsagent's."

"Oh yes, of course." Hornby was still more extravagantly neutral as he came around from behind the counter and peered upward. "Was it *Physique Pictorial, All Male,* or *Muscle Monthly* you were after?"

"I'd really like to have all three, ducky, because you can't have too much of a good thing, can you? Still, the old ready is in short supply, so I'll just take *All Male.*"

"I hear you're not too well," said Hornby, holding out his change. "I'm sorry."

"Oh, don't be. We're all suffering from the same thing, and in the end it always proves fatal. It's called life."

As the sequence ended Hamish turned, reassumed his natural real-life role as an unusually vicious heterosexual, and turning to Melvin Settle, just offset, said, "That is the most corny and sick-making line I've ever had to speak on television. I suppose it's one of yours, is it, Melvin? One of your concentrated essences of worldly wisdom scattered before this nation's yobs and dimwits? It has the ring of you, the mark of your pen. Tell me it's one of your calendar maxims, meant to give the nation its daily ration of thought."

"You're right as always, Hamish," said Melvin quietly. "It's one of the truisms I learned at my mother's knee."

"A knee worn out by scrubbing other people's linoleum, I suppose?"

"How you do hit the nail on the head, Hamish. And how I wish I could return the compliment by hitting a nail into your head."

Permission to film at Leeds-Bradford airport had been given to *Jubilee Terrace* only for one of the less busy weekdays well after the summer rush, so that Cyril's arrival back in the soap had to be filmed much later than the scenes in which his personality had been reestablished and his predicament made known. The script and direction departments were clear in their minds that the scene had to be the airport: a scene at the station, implying that he'd flown to Heathrow or Manchester and then changed mode of transport, was somehow not at all as dramatic as the impossibly dire flight from San Francisco to Leeds. So Lady Wharton and one or two other *Terrace* notables were in the public area just beyond Customs, joining a queue of real relatives meeting loved ones, and extras. Cameras were discreet but everyone, especially the members of the public, were aware of them.

"Darling, don't make me throw my arms around him," pleaded Lady Wharton to Reggie.

"Don't be silly, Winnie. Of course his mother will throw her arms around her son."

"Couldn't I, just before my arms touch him, register how sick he is looking and back away in horror?"

The thought had never occurred to Reggie before.

"Hmmm. I suppose it could work," he said.

"Of course it would. The first thing a mother would do would be to register how her son looked."

"Maybe you're right. Well, we'll try it both ways; then we can choose later."

"Yuck!" said Winnie.

At that moment, after several families had gone past and been greeted by relatives (they were actually off a flight from Paphos), the figure of Cyril was seen walking daintily through the door from Customs. His hair was dyed blond, his luggage was one leather bag carried over his shoulder, and he was wearing a T-shirt with *San Francisco, capital of Gayana* printed on it.

"Cyril!" shouted Winnie, for once getting a line right.

"Mumsie," said Cyril, with a lack of enthusiasm both real and appropriate. She had pulled herself up one foot from actually touching him.

"Darling—you look—"

"I know, Mumsie. Washed out. *Drained.* I'm perfectly all right. If you'd done fourteen hours of ghastly food, ghastly films, and even ghastly classical music, you'd feel like death too. In a couple of days I'll be right as rain."

"Are you sure, darling—?"

But Cyril was looking around at the Terracers who had—without zest—accompanied Winnie to the airport.

"Oh, people," he said ungratefully.

"Yes, darling. Isn't it lovely of them? You know every-one—"

But something had caught Cyril's eye.

"Cut," said Reggie. "Now we'll go back and—"

On his first word Cyril had begun pushing his way past Gladys Porter, past Peter Kerridge and Arthur Bradley, and as he pushed he was becoming not Cyril any longer but Hamish, and the people watching him shed their *Ter-*

race personae as the scene enacted itself before their eyes.

Standing beside a magazine kiosk selling magazines was Bet Garrett. She was there as herself, not as Rita Somerville, the flower-shop owner she played on her rare appearances in the soap. On her face was a smile—one of anticipation, which added nothing of pleasantness or humor to her appearance.

"Darling," shouted Hamish with abundant enthusiasm. "You didn't tell me you were coming!"

"I thought I'd see you welcomed back to the *Terrace*," shouted Bet. "And it seemed a good time—"

"It is! A wonderful time! Couldn't be better." He turned to the assembled public, extras, and fellow cast members. "Be happy for us, all you lot. We're engaged to be married."

There was first silence, then a stunned babble:

"But you can't—"

"Oh yes, we can. You just watch us!"

That night Marjorie Harcourt-Smith sat in the flat she owned in Headingley (where the neighbors congratulated themselves on having a nationally known figure among them, not one of the dreaded students who infested every other street and alleyway in that unfortunate Leeds suburb) and poured herself a third glass of white wine.

Marjorie was puzzled. She had been, in the scene that took place at Leeds-Bradford airport, no more than an extra. After Cyril and Lady Wharton had got into Philip Kerridge's car, she and Arthur had been filmed going toward Arthur's car, and Gladys Porter had had the momentous line "Doesn't he look sick?" One of Marjorie's less memorable days of filming.

But what worried Marjorie was her reaction to Cyril. She had been consumed with hatred for him. Not for Hamish, but for the character Hamish played. She had never had any homophobic prejudices. She didn't now. Yet as the scene had been played out she was conscious that she intensely disliked Cyril. Why? What reason could she give herself? He was, in character, a stage designer of limited talents; he was intent on finding himself a working-class lover (or had been before he went off to America), but both here and probably there he had failed to find any "rough trade"; he was both in thrall to his mother yet on occasion rude and dismissive of her. None of these was a very dreadful trait, none of them a cause for hatred.

And yet she suspected that the character of ineffectual, pathetic Cyril had somehow become merged in her mind with that of the all-too-effectual and constantly aggressive Hamish. When she remembered Cyril confiding the fact of his illness to his old mother she hated him because, behind the makeup and the assumed persona, she always saw the vile Hamish. In this, as Hamish's fellow participant in an apparently endless saga of conflicting personalities, she was perhaps more fortunate than the average viewer who knew not Hamish, perhaps less so.

She wondered, not quite idly, if, supposing Hamish was ever murdered, it would be Hamish or Cyril who was the intended victim.

CHAPTER 4

At Home

✳

Garry Kopps, who played corner shop owner Arthur Bradley in *Jubilee Terrace*, sat at home in the Leeds suburb of Cookridge. He had learned his lines for the next day—something he was expert at—and had written two pages of his projected work on British and Australian soaps, their moral, social, and psychological assumptions. Garry had a huge library of videos, going back twenty years or more, and taking in crucial and fruitful episodes of *EastEnders, Coronation Street, Emmerdale, Albion Market, Casualty,* and even the afternoon soap *Doctors*, as well as *Neighbours* and *Home and Away* from Down Under. And of course his own home territory of *Jubilee Terrace*. The head of scripts, Melvin Settle, had said of his work that it was a deep survey into a shallow pond. And he had added the comment: "Which is impossible." It was a judgment Garry could only agree with.

He got up from his desk and went through into the living room, settling into an easy chair for the Friday episode of *EastEnders*.

Half an hour later, after a continuous diet of raised voices and barely suppressed violence, his notebook was richer by three quotes and two comments on the series' social prejudices. He breathed a sigh of relief and opened a bottle of wine. He had just taken his first sip when the bell from his father's room upstairs rang in the kitchen. Garry put down his drink and hurried up.

"Anything wrong, Dad?"

The gaunt figure on the bed creased his forehead.

"I don't know . . . I forget . . . What time is it?"

"It's just after eight. I've just finished watching *East-Enders*."

"That's nice. Is it a play? . . . It's Sunday, isn't it?"

"No, it's not Sunday, Dad. It's Friday. Now, it's time you settled down and had a really good sleep."

When he was back downstairs he took a deep breath, then an equally big intake of red wine. He loved his father, and continued to love him during his long decline into senility. He always said it was no drag on him to look after him. If he wanted to go away on holiday he took him down to his sister's in Stockport. For short periods away he could get a nurse in. It was no trouble, he always said.

And yet. And yet.

The BBC was currently casting for a new dramatization of *Dombey and Son*. One of Andrew Davies's marvelous jobs. Garry would love to try for the role of Mr. Carker. He had pretty good teeth, a requisite for the role. But what he really wanted to do was to humanize Dickens's cardboard villain—stagey, two-dimensional, unworthy of the rest of the novel.

But he would not put himself forward. After an initial hour-long episode it would be done in twelve half-hour ones. Filming would take months, and it would be shot in London and Broadstairs, with some Continental filming if the budget ran to it. No go. Just too much disruption for Dad. He could square it with his bosses at Northern Television, but not with his conscience. Dad couldn't just be moved in and out of a nursing home as filming dictated, and if he put him in for the whole four months he could easily die there.

No, it was just impossible. Anyway he probably wouldn't have got the job. Saying he wanted to make the character three-dimensional was to cover only the first stage of the process. It was the later stages that were difficult—what was to replace the character's staginess? How in the world was it to be done?

It was becoming the same with Garry's personal life: for much of the time the difficulties deterred him from having one. "I'm just in the way," Tony had said when he moved out. "Your mind is always in there with your dad." And even one of his one-night stands, a lovely boy with natural fair hair that made his heart stop, said he felt like the vegetables that accompanied the meat course. That was when Garry had tried, without much hope, to make him stay a night longer.

The truth was that *Jubilee Terrace* was a bolt-hole: a job that went on and on and engaged only a tiny part of his acting skills. When he was going through drama school he had played Pinchwife in *The Country Wife*. Dad had come to see it—of course—and had found the play a bit "saucy" but thought Garry's performance was "champion." That was typical Dad: other parents would sweat blood to prevent one of their children going to drama school, but Dad had been behind him all the way. He could have done so much better for himself, even in the cutthroat world of the current theater. "I could have been a contender," he muttered with the Brando steaming mumble. He had been National or Royal Shakespeare material.

"Sez me," he immediately came back with. Small parts maybe. Never good ones, interesting ones. Macduff, not Macbeth, Brabantio not Iago.

Three hours and a bottle of wine later, his father's bell rang again. If he waited five minutes his father would turn over and go to sleep. But he downed the dregs of his glass and went quickly up the stairs.

"How did you get this dump?" asked Bet Garrett, as she and Hamish lay looking at the ceiling, for want of anything else to look at.

"It's not a dump. It's a nice small house built in the last few years."

"That's what I mean by a dump."

"It's owned by Northern Television, our respected employers, and they let it out to short- or medium-term actors and such riffraff artists as come within their trawling nets."

"Well, I suppose it's better than a flat over a shop in Albion Street," admitted Bet.

Hamish was in a musing mood.

"Artistes," he said. "That's a word I should have used. I wonder why it has fallen into disuse. It's just the word for the sort of people Northern Television puts into its houses and flats. Not really serious artists, but slightly tacky, slightly tawdry ones. The alternative is one of the Identikit new hotels."

"Mind what you're saying. You're admitting you're one of the tacky ones."

"As long as I'm in a soap I fit the bill exactly. And so do you, my dear."

"I am not tacky."

"You are the most tacky—wonderfully tacky—person I know. You dropped out of drama school, clung to the fringes of theater by marrying someone who can at least do the basics, and can do a tiny bit of reinvention of himself to fill a part in a long-running soap. At least Bill is—just—an actor. If you had a regular role people would begin to notice that they saw over and over again the same facial expressions, the same body language—shrugs, hand gestures, tosses of the head. You are an artiste, my dear, the sort of person who gets recognized in a supermarket once a month, and usually by someone who can't put a name to you—not your real one or your soap one."

Bet screwed up her lip in an ugly pout.

"Thanks very much. I see why everyone calls you a shit."

"Watch it, madam. Though since I'm doing shit work for you I suppose that is the aspect of my many-faceted character that you would fix on."

Bet giggled, a sound at once dirty and vengeful.

"You jumped at the chance, you know you did."

"I've nothing against Bill that I can remember. And I *would* remember. I suppose I don't like sturdy, trustworthy men that aging actresses love to rely on, take their troubles to. In real life Bill would be the pivotal figure in a school staff room, the shoulder to weep on in the works canteen. He's the one everyone drops by on, to have a word in his ear. Silly oaf—wasting his time pretending to solve other people's insoluble problems. That is about as useful as spending money on a lottery ticket or a scratch card. You don't ever get thanks for it, though you get plenty of blame when things go pear-shaped."

"Poor old Bill," said Bet, with that giggle again. "Everything in his life has turned pear-shaped at the moment."

"Especially his marriage, obviously . . . Want a drink?"

"If nothing better's on offer."

"It isn't. Once is enough. I'm the prostitute here. You want more, you pay for it."

"As if I would . . . Are you getting lots of congratulations on our engagement?"

"As if I would. I'm the *Terrace*'s pariah. No one talks to me if they don't have to. What about you?"

"No, of course I'm not." She put out her hand to take her brandy and soda. Hamish knew her druthers. "Anyway, I've only had a couple of hours filming so far since the announcement. And they all love Bill, like you say . . . But I'm a bit afraid that no one is taking the engagement seriously."

"That would be a pity. Especially if Bill embraced the general skepticism."

Bet indulged in what passed for thought in her.

"Yes, I have wondered. But he can't be *sure*, can he? He will be in a permanent state of uncertainty. And then he'll hear from my solicitor that I'm claiming custody of the girls. That will be the last thing he expects. And he'll wonder whether I'm marrying you to strengthen my claim on them."

"I'm not normally regarded as the sort who would strengthen anyone's claim on anything. Still, I think you're right. He'll be unable to be *sure* about anything, and it will drive him up the wall. And the fact that I'm in the picture, and the picture includes *his* girls—it will be absolute torment for the poor chap. I like the thought."

Hamish laughed.

"I like it too," said Bet.

"Poor old tormented, child-fixated Bill. I'm going to enjoy seeing his face when I'm around."

"Me too. That's what this is all about."

"They say he's fixated these days on that snotty little juvenile Susan Fyldes."

"First I've heard of it. Nobody talks to me, any more than they do to you. By the look of her he'll never get very far. She'll use her sex for an upward curve through the acting profession. Bill was never any sort of upward curve."

"No one will ever get anywhere with her," Hamish said. "Not if they expect emotion to be involved. It will be pure calculation. She'll be very conscious of the ultimate Maginot Line, and sex will be part of her credit card journey to the top. Poor old Vernon Watts found that out."

"Vernon? I never knew that he was interested."

"Oh, but he was. During my first stint as Cyril. Always snuffling and wheezing around Susan, and getting nowhere. You can just see a glorious creature like Susan (as she imagines herself to be) having anything to do with a clapped-out old music-hall star, can't you? Quite turns the stomach, thinking of her and Vernon Watts in bed together."

"Hamish, do you like *any*one?"

Hamish shrugged his shoulders.

"Not that I can remember offhand . . . Sometimes I think I could like some of the people I see on TV, but I expect I'd hate them if I met them in what is humorously called real life."

"We're splendidly matched. I don't like anyone either."

"Not even your fine set of daughters?"

"Especially not my set of miniature harpies. If it came to the worst, my getting custody, I'd dump them on my mother as fast as I could."

"What kind of a woman is your mother?"

"People often say I'm a chip off the old block." They both laughed. "The girls would survive. They're tough. They've had to be."

"I'm sorry I won't be around to see it."

"Who says you won't be around to see it?"

He threw back his head at her stupidity.

"I'm incurably ill, remember? *Cyril* is incurably ill. I'm on a four-month contract—they've got it calculated to a nicety. And the mills of the law grind slowly, with your own solicitor seeming to manage a particularly slow grind."

"We could always *get* married, so you could keep up your interest in the girls."

"I have no interest in the girls. I hope you're not trying to make out that I—"

"No, of course I wasn't."

"Then any other sort of interest is definitely not worth the expense of a wedding. This engagement is *just* a move to have a laugh at Bill's expense—right?"

"Right."

But Bet still thought it was a pity. She and Hamish were in so many ways suited.

James Selcott put down the phone and lay back on his bed. Another rejection. A polite one, regretful, hoping she would be free next time he rang. But a rejection nonetheless.

It didn't really worry him, he told himself. He could go along to a club any time he liked, pick up a girl for sex any time he liked. In his life the club was more important than the sex. At a club he could be looked at, watched, *admired.* He was the center of his own life, and no one was ever going to push him to its sidelines.

James knew he had what it took to make a great actor. One day, and that day soon, he was going to be asked to audition for the National or the Royal Shakespeare. That invitation would not be the result of his playing Will Brown in *Jubilee Terrace,* but of the small slots he worked on in his times out of the soap—one-acters at lunchtime theaters in London, companies that sprang up, had a coterie success on the Edinburgh Festival fringes, then faded as quickly as tropical blooms. Soon the notices he got in the *Guardian* and the *Independent on Sunday* would pay off, and he would slough off the *Terrace* as if it were an unwanted skin.

What it took to be a great actor (returning to an earlier

thought) was self-absorption, tunnel vision, the ability to absorb a fictitious role and weld it into his own personality. Over the eighteen months of his appearing in *Jubilee Terrace*, Will Brown, his character, had changed, and recently he had become less likeable by the episode. James was quite conscious of this. James didn't do likeable.

What James did was single-mindedness. He was destined for a career of outstanding distinction because he was the foremost young actor of his generation. Fuck that incredible twerp Hamish Fawley who'd suggested he'd gone into acting when he'd failed to get into plumbing. He'd show Hamish. He'd ram his distinction as an actor down Hamish's throat till he choked. That'd be the only suitable punishment for him. James was quite happy to be disliked, but he couldn't tolerate being despised, or—most difficult of all to forgive—being condescended to.

In her Northern Television flat in Pudsey—recently decorated with no taste whatsoever—Susan Fyldes cooked herself a Marks & Spencer frozen meal for one and began planning her evening.

She was going to Marco's Place with Stephen, Mariella, June, Richard, Halvard, and Wayne. All of them except Wayne were young people her parents would have approved of. They were of "the right sort," and if they, her parents, were unaware of some of the things their daughter's group did, or things that they took—well, ignorance was bliss, and Susan was the last person in the world to enlighten their darkness.

Wayne was perhaps—no, not perhaps, definitely—well

beneath their class, but he was a lovely boy, and had worshiped her from the moment she walked onto his TV
screen on her first appearance in *Jubilee Terrace*. So
Wayne came along on most of their clubbing nights, and
provided a willing pair of ears for Susan's tales of her family's past: how her grandfather had been Lord Lieutenant
of West Yorkshire, how her great-great-grandmother had
been the mistress of the Duke of Edinburgh ("not the
present one, of course," she would say with a giggle, "but
Queen Victoria's second son"), how an uncle had been a
top civil servant in the Ministry of Agriculture, and a second cousin a mannequin with Hardy Amies. All these
claims were, so far as Susan knew, true, but people had
been known to be less than impressed by them. Wayne,
dear old Wayne, drank them in and asked for more.

Of course these days a lot of people professed to be
indifferent to claims of family distinction. You are what
you are, they tended to say, not what your great-great relatives and ancestors were. Susan thought people like
that were just jealous. Anyway, she had more than proved
her worth in her own right—proved it every weekday
night, when *Jubilee Terrace* was broadcast. She didn't
need ancestors, though she certainly loved to talk about
them.

Hamish's jibe about apprentice plumbers still rankled.

Winnie Hey put a saucepan of milk on the hot plate and
spooned Ovaltine into a cup. She liked a drink at the end
of the day, but not an alcoholic one, which had the opposite effect on her to that it had on most people: it kept
her awake.

Philip Marston had rung in the early evening to see if she wanted to come out to the pub. She often enjoyed being with a little knot of *Terrace* people who drank regularly at The Palace: she thought the other actors enjoyed her tales of rep disasters in the fifties and sixties—and if they didn't they were good at hiding the fact. She enjoyed their vitality and optimism—so different from the stale and bitter cynicism of Hamish. But she knew Philip asked her more from a sense of social correctness than anything else: she had once heard him say, "The old are people like the rest of us," and she'd thought grimly, Until they start losing all the things that make them individual. She enjoyed pub nights, was grateful for being asked, but tried to refuse often enough not to become a fixture.

She sat in her chair in the two-roomed flat in The Calls, bought before prices had gone through the roof but when they were already touching the ceiling. She was happy, satisfied, almost complacent. The end of Cyril was in sight, which meant a final farewell to Hamish. And what made her complacent was that nobody had suggested that Lady Wharton would move away from her inappropriately working-class flat in Jubilee Terrace. And why should she? She had friends there, things to do. If she, Winnie, had been a Lady Wharton she would have stayed on. The enchanting prospect was rising before her of employment until death, or until the dreaded nursing home became an inevitability.

She had during the last years had a fantasy of being in a nursing home and acting as executioner to all who offended her morals or her tastes: gropers, lovers of

Radio One, greedy coveters of other people's unconsidered trifles. It would be so easy in a nursing home to kill someone, several someones, because people were dying all the time. She felt sure she could ram tablets down their throats while they were asleep, or even while they were in their usual comatose condition.

Her fantasy of killing Hamish had become less vividly real as his departure date came nearer. Pity, really, because it had been a good idea, and, like all those people she would enjoy bumping off in her old-people's home, it presented itself to her as an act of social and moral sanitation: benefiting all by an act that improved the quality of their lives.

Yes, it was a shame that she would no longer be called upon to rescue people in advance from having to endure the agony of acting in a play, film, or soap whose cast was also graced by that moral leper Hamish.

But of course she'd never been serious, had she?

Bet Garrett pushed open the door of her own semi-detached home—or what had until recently been that—and listened. Not a sound. The girls were still at school, and she'd ascertained the fact that Bill would be filming. She hauled her empty suitcases into the hall and went upstairs to the bedroom she had shared (on and off) with Bill. She pulled out the drawers in the dressing table and left the doors of the wardrobe open so she could simply grab the most desirable items and bundle them in the cases. There was no guarantee, she told herself, that Bill would not take all that remained and give them to one of the charity shops.

She was happily, if haphazardly, engaged in filling the larger case when she became aware of a face at the door.

"Christ, Debbie, you made me jump. What the hell are you doing home?" She gave another, lesser jump when another face appeared behind the first. "Rosie! What is this? What's that f-ing useless father of yours mean by letting you wag school?"

"We're not wagging school," said Debbie. "It's half term."

"How was I supposed to know that when nobody told me?"

"You haven't been around to tell," said the third figure to appear at the door. "And Dad's not useless."

"Well, he's obviously using you as an unpaid child-minder."

That was rich, Angela thought.

"I've been an unpaid child-minder since I was five. And I've never asked for pay from you, so I don't see why I should from Dad."

"Oh, have it your own way. It's not for me to worry about you now." The children remained silent. Leaving them alone had never worried her in the past. "Well, I think that's all I can manage at the moment. Tell your dad I'll be back for one more installment, then he can do what he likes with whatever's left."

"I expect he'll put it out with the garbage," said Angela.

"Oh, do you, young lady? Well, if he was the caring, sharing bugger he pretends to be he'd take it to a charity shop, or give it to the Sally Army. Too much trouble, I suppose. Well, he'll see what trouble three small monsters like you are, won't he? I suppose I should say, 'Be good,' but I won't bother because I hope you give him hell."

She clicked her case shut with a ringing finality, then pushed past the two younger ones, gave a look of particular dislike at her eldest, then humped the suitcases down the stairs. As she came to the hall she stopped and picked up an envelope from the little table.

"I missed this. When did it come?"

"This morning," Angela said. "Dad had already gone."

"My bloody solicitor, getting his finger out at last. Well, tell your dad I mean every word. He's not getting his way over this—why should he?"

And not specifying what she was talking about, she threw open the front door and banged it shut behind her. Angela went and looked at the envelope. The inscription in the top left-hand corner read, "Bland, Witterley and Kemble, Solicitors." She easily opened the self-adhesive envelope.

Later that day, when Bill arrived home, Angela left him to himself for a quarter of an hour, as she often did, then went down to talk to him. She found him on the sofa in the sitting room, his head in his hand, sobbing. The letter was on the rug in front of him. She ran over and put her arms around him.

"Dad! Dad! She doesn't mean it! She was here today. I know she doesn't mean it. She doesn't want anything to do with us. She made that quite clear."

Bill dabbed a handkerchief to his eyes.

"Oh, I know that, my darling. I know she couldn't care less about you. But that's what I'm afraid of: that some damn fool of a judge will give custody of you to someone who doesn't give a damn about you."

CHAPTER 5

Deathbed Scene

✳

Charlie Peace looked at Reggie Friedman and Melvin Settle and he saw in their faces nothing but bewilderment. They studied his ID card—*Detective Inspector Dexter A. Peace*—as if it were a piece of dog dirt found on the immaculately maintained set of *Jubilee Terrace*.

"Yes?" said Melvin Settle, with a combination of hauteur and condescension.

"We have received an anonymous letter," began Charlie, conscious it was not a brilliant opening.

"Oh? Don't the police normally suggest that such garbage is thrown straight in the bin where it belongs?"

"Sometimes we do. Since this one concerns a national figure—though a very minor one—we thought we could be in deep trouble with the tabloids if we didn't do a certain amount of investigation."

"Oh, the tabloids," said Reggie, as if the last thing Northern Television would pay attention to was the *Sun* or the *Mirror*. "And *what* national figure, might I ask?"

"The letter named an actor called Vernon Watts—" began Charlie. The result stopped him in his tracks.

"Christ Almighty," said Reggie. "He's been dead more than four months."

"—who played the part of Bert Porter, I believe."

"He did, yes." Reggie looked at his watch. "Look here, Melvin, I've got to be at a script conference. Could you take over here?"

"You seem to forget, Reggie"—the voice was oiled and urbane—"that my work title is script editor in chief. I chair all script conferences."

"Oh, I know, Melvin, but we're in agreement on all the main subjects so I can easily chair this one in your absence."

"I shan't be absent, Reggie. The matter of this new curate and whether the part should be developed is coming up. It's a tricky business. A vicar is all very well in *Emmerdale,* and long ago they had a wet young curate in *EastEnders,* but a lot of people feel that a curate would fit in ill with a North Country soap, even if we manage to make him into a real character." He turned to Charlie. "The meeting won't last more than an hour. Can you amuse yourself for that long?"

Charlie nodded, but they were not looking, and were already ushering him out—pushing would better describe it—and locking the door to Reggie's office, where Charlie had been shown when he had first arrived. As the pair bustled off down the corridor Charlie looked at his watch: eleven twenty. He felt condescended to by that phrase "amuse yourself," but nevertheless he could wander around and see how a soap was made. Alternatively he could leave the studio and look for the nearest pub. His shift was already ten minutes from its end. Or did they serve real beer in the soap's Duke of York? He knew there were regular visits to the studio by the public and fans, chaperoned and kept on the rails by employees of Northern Television.

He decided to opt for the fantasy world, and hope that the alcohol would not turn out to be cold tea. He felt he could do with a chaperone himself, but decided instead to wander on spec, and to home in on any area that voices were coming from. His initial explorations produced little but silent corridors, sometimes containing offices with what he suspected were outrageously overhyped job titles on the door placards. Eventually he landed up in a studio where filming was taking place. The setting was a room with a view (onto redbrick houses forming a terrace), and a bed—not a marital or an extramarital bed, but a sick one. Charlie stood next to an elderly lady who was sitting straight-backed on an upright chair.

"Oh no!" came a voice from the bed. "You've marched bang between me and the camera. It's amateur night all over again. Did you train with the Oswaldtwistle Players? The focus here is on me. I'm dying slowly. It isn't on my spiritual mentor, or would-be mentor. Get it? You'll be lucky if the great unwashed audience ever sees your face."

"I decide where the focus is," came from a man in jeans and trainers by a camera.

"Jim Carrington," explained the elderly lady next to Charlie in a whisper. "Reggie Friedman's second in command. Directs episodes Reggie doesn't want to do or can't."

"I'm sure you had to learn the tricks of the trade when you started in television," said the youthful figure in a dog collar and flannels. "I'm learning as quickly as I can. Try to exercise a bit of charity."

"Christ Almighty!" said Hamish Fawley, obviously suspecting a tongue in cheek, and rightly. "He'll be sending in his application for the Archbishopric of Canterbury next."

The edge of humor in the "curate's" intervention pleased Charlie, though he was not sure if the young actor's "taking the piss" was aimed at Hamish or at his own role as wet-behind-the-ears curate.

"He's new," came the elderly woman's voice. Charlie looked down at her and liked what he saw.

"I think I've seen you in the show," he said. "With a different voice."

"Oh, the different voice goes without saying," she said. "My father was manager of the City Varieties for three years back in the forties, so of course we lived in Leeds. Yorkshire comes quite naturally to me, and I've never lost it. It's been useful over the years, and luckily Gladys Porter is not meant to be broad."

"Ah yes, Gladys Porter," said Charlie, who had perhaps seen *Jubilee Terrace* a dozen times.

"I'm Marjorie Harcourt-Smith. Are you auditioning for a new part?"

"Auditioning? No. Do I look like an actor? I'm flattered."

"I don't see why you should be flattered. It's only slavery with the added disadvantage of frequent unemployment."

"I'm flattered because in television drama everybody is twenty-five percent better looking than his or her equivalent in real life and twenty-five percent better dressed as well. Anyway you've already got your token black, haven't you?"

They both looked to the other end of the studio, where Susan and James, ever together and ever apart, were sprawled in two easy chairs.

"Oh, we don't have token blacks—I mean, we've had lots in the past: Mr. Raschid the garage proprietor and . . ." Her voice and memory failed her. "Yes, we have one token black. For the moment."

"Not popular?"

"A right little shit. You don't mind my saying so?"

"Not at all. All minorities have the right to produce shits. Or even monsters. Anyway, I'm Charlie Peace." He got out his ID. "Inspector Peace."

Marjorie Harcourt-Smith peered at the plastic.

"Inspector? Health and Safety?"

"No, law and order."

"Oh, good heavens." Charlie watched her eyebrows going skyward. "Well, you'd know all about tokenism."

"You were married—in the soap—to Vernon Watts, weren't you?"

There was a throb in the voice when she simply said, "Yes."

"What sort of man was he?"

"Look, we were about as close as those two over there. Not close at all. You won't get a balanced account from me."

"Well, I'll settle for an unbalanced one. So far I have nothing on him."

"Well—" She stopped before she started. "But why are you interested in Vernon?"

"Never mind that. Just tell me about him, and why you didn't get on."

Marjorie closed her eyes.

"He was an aging music-hall star. Made a good living for a time in the variety theaters and working men's clubs. Got used to the spotlight, loved it and needed it. Then when the music hall faded—"

Charlie felt out of his depth and held up an open hand to stop her.

"What exactly *was* the music hall, and why did it fade?"

"Song and dance, conjurors, acrobats, even hypnotists. What the Americans called vaudeville but music hall lasted longer. Comics like Vernon were its backbone. It faded because of radio and television. *Hancock's Half Hour, Round the Horne.* Then television sitcoms like *Steptoe and Son* and *Dad's Army*. The music hall couldn't cope with that class of competition. It became surplus to requirements. Vernon was enormously lucky to get the part of Bert Porter. Not that he ever showed any consciousness of his luck, let alone gratitude for it."

"I'm beginning to get the picture," said Charlie. "We've just heard one of your current actors throwing a hissy fit. Were there resemblances?"

"Between Hamish and Vernon? Oh, please—I wouldn't want you to think Vernon was that bad. Hamish is a one-off. Vernon was vain, he was pushy, he tried to sleep with all the new girls in the series—"

"Did he succeed?"

"Not recently. All the new girls were tipped the wink that if they thought sleeping with Vernon might be a way of getting a permanent role in *Terrace* they should think again. Boys were warned too, because Vernon was not averse to a change of scenery."

"Boys like your handsome black friend over there?"

"Oh, James wouldn't need a warning. He's got everything sized up and summed up. He'll know exactly who's worth cultivating, and how. There's just one drawback for James."

"What's that?"

"He's not interested in making it in a soap. He wants to be a great actor. He wants to make his mark in *Jubilee Terrace,* then move onwards and upwards."

"And will he?"

Marjorie shrugged.

"Who can say? He has the drive and the ego. But people suspect that everything he does acquires a little strain of James. And James is not nice. That's a problem, if your nastiness is unsuppressible. It's appropriate if you're playing a young Hannibal Lecter, not appropriate at all if you're playing Othello or some heroic goodie like John Proctor in *The Crucible* or Ibsen's *Enemy of the People.*"

"Not parts susceptible to a takeover by James's real character, I take it," said Charlie, vowing to run all this over with his wife. Felicity would understand the psychology.

"Not at all. Why don't you go over and talk to him?"

"I think I will. Is this dying scene in the can?"

"It's not a dying scene. That's next week. No, there'll probably be one final take—Jim's preparing for it now."

But there was a change of plan. Jim Carrington came up to his two actors and put his hand on the curate's shoulder.

"I think that will do. Well done, both of you. What I have in mind now is to do a quick run-through of the death scene. Deaths are always big news in soaps, and we have to be careful to get it right. Are you up in the lines, Stephen?"

"Pretty well," said the polite, almost prissy voice. "I'll be near enough."

Jim turned to his problem actor.

"You don't have much, Hamish, but it's very important. We'll film; then we can go over the rushes to see what needs polishing up. Can we take it from 'Have you thought about what we talked over last week?'"

Stephen, the miracle recruit, let the lines come out from his clerical lips as though they were coming from the infinitely patient lips of a teacher of a naughty child.

"No, I haven't," said Hamish as Cyril. "What's the point? I don't believe, and that's that."

"Many people feel, as the end approaches—"

"Death. It's called death."

"—as death approaches, that the spiritual side of things becomes more important, and they have a quite different take on the afterlife."

"I don't believe in an afterlife."

"Let's just say 'what comes after this one.'"

"Nothing does. Zilch. If I was to start believing in God

and an afterlife now, it would be like taking out an insurance policy on a house that's already fallen down."

"Well, I won't force anything on you. Let's just sit and think for a moment." The curate put his hand on Cyril's hand, lying on the embroidered eiderdown. "Do you feel any difference? Is it coming?" There was silence, then Cyril said, "Yes. Yes—I do feel something coming."

"Try to help it. Welcome it."

The camera honed in on the hands on the bed. Slowly Cyril's hand turned over, then it grasped the curate's. For almost a minute it held it tight. Then suddenly relaxed.

Jim let the cameras dwell on the two hands. Then he was ecstatic.

"That was brilliant. Sometimes first rehearsals can be so much fresher than final takes."

"We'll have to have a change in the dialogue," said Hamish, leaping out of bed and revealing jeans under his pajama top. "We can't have all this 'Is it coming?' It sounds as if he's reaching the end of a long spell of constipation."

"You both did it so beautifully I don't think anyone will think that," said Jim.

"We could perhaps alter it to 'a change coming,'" suggested Stephen Barrymore.

"Oh great," sneered Hamish. "Make it sound as if homosexuals go through the menopause as well as women. Stick to acting, feller, which you're least bad at."

"The trouble with the English language is that practically every word has an indecent connotation," said Jim. "Hence the dreadful puns in the tabloids. Well, we'll have to see what we can do about it, if any change is needed. That about winds things up for this morning."

Charlie shifted his weight from foot to foot, having been deeply absorbed in this death scene. He raised his hand to Marjorie, then set off around the edge of the studio toward the far end. He was interrupted by a call from Jim.

"I say. You there. Do you have a pass to be here?"

"I think so," said Charlie, going over. He flipped out his ID and held it in front of Jim's face. Jim looked disconcerted.

"But I say. Police. I mean, what—? Am I allowed to ask what it is you're here on?"

"Certainly you're allowed to ask, and in this case I'll tell you. I'm here to investigate a matter which has arisen as a consequence of an anonymous letter to the police. I'm talking to Mr. Friedman and Mr. Settle after their script conference. Now, if you don't mind . . ."

And he continued on his way. He was conscious of many eyes following him—not just Jim Carrington's, but Hamish's, Stephen Barrymore's, the cameramen's, and most intently of all James's and Susan's from the far wall of the studios.

"What did you show Jim?" demanded Susan when he reached them.

"Show him?"

"Flash at him," said James. "Like an identity card."

"It *was* an identity card," said Charlie, showing it to the pair of them. "Satisfied?"

"Well, well," said James, stirring up trouble as was his

wont. "A black policeman. Wonders will never cease. What are you: a traitor or a stooge?"

"Well, well, a black actor in a soap. I'll hold back on the supplementary questions."

"If you're a policeman you must be investigating something," said Susan.

"If you only knew how much time I spend *not* investigating . . . But today's not one of those times. Let me jump ahead and say it's an investigation prompted by an anonymous letter we received at police headquarters. It made allegations that we thought needed looking into."

"What sort of allegations?" asked James.

"Shall I do the questioning? How long have you been working on *Jubilee Terrace*, sir?"

"Eighteen months, or a bit over."

"And you, madam?"

Charlie gave their honorary titles a gently ironic tinge.

"Nearly four years. I've been given bigger and better things to do since I finished at drama school."

"Who would you say has been most helpful to you since you started?"

The pair thought.

"Melvin is a very good scriptwriter," said Susan. "If I have trouble with a line, maybe think that a teenager wouldn't say it, Melvin is—"

"Yes, I've met Melvin Settle," said Charlie. "And you, sir?"

James shrugged.

"I've just got on with the job. It's not—"

"Rocket science. Yes, I get the point. What about the people who've been less helpful? The ones you wouldn't think of going to if you had a problem. The ones who are a problem?"

"Well," said Susan, "you've just seen Hamish, and what he can do to a newcomer. Crude, nasty, but depressing all the same, and confidence-robbing. Vernon Watts was the elderly groper in the cast. I gave him his marching orders on my first day. I had a sort of chaperone then, but she was surplus to requirements. I can take care of myself."

Charlie turned to James and waited.

"Oh, I was approached by Vernon too. Could have guessed he was into variety. I told him I wasn't into being fucked by wrinklies. Hamish has tried a few sneers in the Vernon Watts mode. It's all water off a duck's back. I know where I'm going. Vernon must have known where he was going too, and now he's gone."

"Don't take any notice of him."

Charlie swiveled around and noticed a little band of actors and studio-hands gazing at them. The actors included Marjorie, the young curate, and a fresh-faced woman of an age somewhere between youth and middle-age.

"You are?"

"I'm Liza Croome. I play Sally Worseley in the *Terrace*. Wife of the landlord of the Duke of York's."

"And you don't like the way James is talking about Vernon Watts and Hamish Whatever?"

"Fawley. I just think he's giving a wrong impression. James is . . . still quite new here. On the whole this is a wonderful team. We all—nearly all—pull together extremely well. We're actors, bumped-up extras, comedians, whatever. And we do play together, hide one another's weaknesses, highlight their strengths. The tabloids say what a united and close-knit lot we are, and on the whole they're right. In this case any rotten apple there may have been hasn't affected the whole barrel."

"God's in his heaven, all's right with the world," said James, getting up and walking eloquently away. Charlie watched the walk—all panther grace and glorious, self-conscious elegance. The boy would make a very high-class gigolo, he decided. Suddenly James stopped and turned around. "Liza, you didn't mention that Bill Garrett, your mate, is letching after Susan, did you? Why not? Didn't fit with your rosy picture of the happy cast, I suppose."

"Hello—making yourself at home, I see. Excellent." It was Reggie Friedman, arriving with Melvin Settle and looking with raised eyebrows at the departing back of James. The welcoming note had got into Reggie's bearing and stance, but Charlie noticed there was still an edge to his voice. "If you'll come along we'll give you all the help we can."

They led Charlie not to the office where they had talked earlier, but to one of the *Terrace's* hospitality suites, where they sat in light, clean easy chairs, and where a coffee machine was already switched on and biscuits were neatly arranged on plates. Something had happened in the script conference, Charlie thought, or, more likely, the two men had thought things over and decided that nothing could be gained by stonewalling or offending a police officer. And perhaps particularly a black police officer, since the *Terrace* had not, over the years, been very welcoming to minorities. Maybe in this thinking his inspector title had helped. The rank was always more impressive to outsiders than it was to other serving policemen, who knew that inspectors usually got the rather boring cases.

"So you've had an anonymous letter," said Reggie Friedman, sitting down and gesturing to another chair. "You said it was about Vernon Watts?"

"Exactly."

"Was it from a member of the public, do you think, or from one of our people here?"

"From a *Jubilee Terrace* insider, we thought, or someone close to an insider."

"Many of our fans are so well up in the series, from its start in 1976, that they can sound like insiders."

"Point taken. We're keeping an open mind."

"Are we allowed to know what the letter said?" asked Melvin Settle.

"Yes. I've had it transcribed, and I'd like the copy back." Charlie fumbled in his briefcase and handed over a copy. "We don't want it to go round from person to person so that people can prepare their responses. It was very legibly written, so you can rely on the transcript."

The pair took the single page and looked at the computer text.

Why did the police take Vernon Watt's death as natural causes? He was the most hated man on *Jubilee Terrace*. Pushing someone in front of a car is the easiest way of killing him. The London police should have investigated all the people on the traffic island.

"Hmmm," said Melvin. "Gets the apostrophe wrong in 'Watts's.'"

"Nobody gets that right these days," said Reggie. "Except you, Melvin." He looked at Charlie. "Not much there I'd have said. Of course you know your job best, but . . ."

"You're quite right," said Charlie, with easy candor. "Normally with an anonymous letter, very unspecific and ungrounded, we'd have done nothing. We might have paid some attention if it was signed, and we could question the writer. The unusual thing here, the reason we're taking it up at all, is as I said earlier: that Watts was something of a national figure, partly from his early life on the music halls—"

"But mainly because of *Jubilee Terrace*," said Reggie Friedman.

"I was going to say that. The music halls and the variety shows are, I gather, a happy memory for older people. Even the working men's clubs, which are a Northern phenomenon, are not what they were. So it's for *Jubilee Terrace* Vernon Watts will be remembered. Tell me about the part he played, Bert Porter."

"Oh, Bert was a *Terrace* stalwart. He'd been in the cotton trade, with a sideline as a comic and a vocalist on the club circuit. That way we kept and capitalized on Vernon's showbiz connection. Bert was now retired, with the occasional engagement in clubs or pubs. He and his wife, Gladys, were comfortable, apart from the odd row, and were founts of popular wisdom whenever there was any trouble on the Terrace."

"And there's always trouble on the Terrace," said Melvin.

"Is it true that pushing people under a bus or car is a fail-safe way of getting rid of them?" asked Reggie.

Charlie shrugged.

"If it were that good a way of killing someone, the killing wouldn't be in our records. If people are all around when the killer pushes, it's a lot more risky than our know-it-all letter writer admits. Anyone may see or feel the arm that does the pushing. If it was I, I'd push my victim in front of an underground train in rush hour. Ill-lit platform, great mass of surging humanity. A shove is part of life there."

"Vernon Watts hadn't used the Underground since the 7/7 London terrorist bombings," said Melvin. "He was an asthmatic, and he didn't want to die in a smoke-filled tunnel."

"Ah. Now what about the letter writer's statement that Vernon was the most generally hated actor on the *Terrace* sets?"

"I imagine that's what you may have heard if you've talked to some of the cast," said Reggie. "Well, yes—it was true until Hamish Fawley returned to the show."

"That's the actor I've just seen on his deathbed. I guessed he was dying of AIDS, but I was wrong."

"That's the one. He's dying of tuberculosis. Still, AIDS was a good guess. He's a nasty piece of work and thrives on being nasty. He's just come back for a second stint on the show. Vernon was less nasty, less confident in his brutality to others, but his approach was on the same lines. Just a bit less piercing in his bitchery and malevolence.

The fact that his first career had folded under him may explain the lack of confidence."

"Is Mr. Fawley's main base London?" asked Charlie.

"Well, yes"—Reggie's answer was palpably reluctant—"it is." Charlie waited. "Actually he has a flat in Hampstead, inherited from his parents. He lets it out when he's playing or filming elsewhere, like now."

"And at the time of Watts's death?"

Reluctance again.

"He was in London in *School for Scandal* at the Haymarket Theatre."

"Very interesting," said Charlie.

"May we ask," said Melvin with his usual courtly diffidence, "whether there were signs of a hefty shove on Vernon's back?"

"No, there were not. Otherwise there would have been an inquest. The Metropolitan Police's autopsy showed he had a heart attack but it could have happened either before or after he fell or was pushed into the road. Let me ask you one: Was Mr. Watts a dodderer, or becoming doddery?"

Both men nodded vigorously.

"Oh yes," said Reggie. "Everyone says that back in the past he had limitless energy. When he was on the club circuit Vernon could do half an hour, even three-quarters, as a solo turn: jokes, songs, dance—even some conjuring tricks. You name it, he was in for it. I'm told he still had a lot of that energy when he joined *Jubilee Terrace*, but he'd lost most of it by the time he died. Perhaps that soured his temper. He and Marjorie, who played his wife, had many a slanging match, but their disputes were the main outlet for the energy he had left."

"Not sex?"

"Well, he was still up for it," said Reggie with a leer. "But everyone in the studio knew what he was after, and that he'd make promises about using his influence which he couldn't keep because he had none. He was just a shabby, comic figure."

"But physically he was doddery—no longer firm on his feet, unsure where he was going, what he was doing?"

"Oh yes," said Melvin. "He was *old,* and like all but a few old people. What are you trying to say?"

"I'm not sure," said Charlie. "The physical decline works two ways: he could be projected forward into the path of a car without any difficulty, or without leaving any bruise; on the other hand, he could have just wimbley-wambled himself into the road."

The two men thought this over.

"He wasn't mad," said Melvin, "or even a bit soft in the head. He had all his marbles, and you could hear that in any of the rows he had."

"Nobody has suggested he was mad," said Reggie.

"No, that's right," said Charlie, getting up. "I think we've gone as far as we can go. I didn't expect to get any great distance, but we have put a marker down. If something turns up that makes us think there was anything in this letter writer's allegations then at least we can say we didn't bin them without giving them a go. It's the most the public can expect."

"I'm sure you're right," said Reggie. "Nobody here

thought Vernon's death was anything but an accident or the result of the heart attack."

"Not quite true, Reggie," said Melvin. "Garry Kopps says that the first thing he thought when he heard the news was that Vernon'd been done in."

"Garry's got an overactive imagination," said Reggie.

"And who is Garry Kopps?" asked Charlie.

"Our resident gay—in real life. Also our resident intellectual. In the soap as Arthur Bradley, the keeper of the corner shop."

Charlie nodded, said he'd got everything he needed, and as he left the room said he didn't imagine there would be any reason for him to come back. So much for policeman's instinct.

CHAPTER 6

Aflame

✳

"Good evening, Peter. And how are you this fine evening?" Bob Worseley's arm had gone automatically to the draft Guinness, Philip Marston's regular tipple. "And is the gorgeous Mrs. Kerridge in her usual fine fettle?"

"Cut the crap, Bill. They've not even finalized the camera angles yet. And anyway, your idea of a pub landlord is fatally dated. All you get in a pub these days is a horrible little man with a short-term contract and about as much warmth and bonhomie as the pope receiving an official visit from the Reverend Ian Paisley."

"Everything about *Jubilee Terrace* is dated, right down to white people running the corner shop," said Bill Garrett, unperturbed. "Hadn't you noticed?"

"You're right," said Marjorie Harcourt-Smith, who was sitting with her "sweet sherry" (actually a neat cognac) at a table beside them with Winnie Hey. "How often do you see people in the Terrace talking into their mobile phones or listening to music on their iPods as they walk? Only the teenagers, just occasionally. But go out into the real street and everybody is at it."

"She's hit the nail on the head as usual," said Philip Marston, who loved double meanings. "Go out on the street and everybody is at it."

"Don't turn me into a smut merchant," said Marjorie. "Smut's not your line at all, and not mine either."

"Ah, now this brightens my day," said Bill, polishing a glass. "A new customer at the Duke of York's. What's the betting he drinks orange juice?"

Marjorie and Winnie looked around. All the characters for the pub scene that was shortly to be filmed were already there: Norma Kerridge; Arthur Bradley and his still-new wife, Maureen; the wide-eyed young ingenue Dawn Kerridge, tonight without James, all supervised by Reggie Friedman, being everywhere at once.

And there, over by the door, was the new curate.

"What's he doing here?" asked Marjorie. "He's not in this scene."

"Maybe he is," said Winnie. "Melvin could have done a little rewrite. He was awfully good in those scenes with my Cyril."

"I know he was. I was there," said Marjorie but Winnie was not listening.

"Only a filmed run-through. But *awfully* good, and really very moving. Though maybe I was especially moved because it was the last of Hamish . . . No, I don't think it was that. It was because this youngster's an actor, a real actor."

"Do you know, I don't think I even know his name," said Marjorie, "I just think of him as the curate."

"He's Stephen Barrymore, and he's in his last year at the music and drama college here in Leeds. His *Terrace* name is Kevin Plunkett."

And by then the curate was standing by Winnie's shoulder, talking to Philip Marston and downing a pint.

"I hear you did a good job with Hamish's death scene," said Philip.

"It was just a first run-through, but I thought it hit the right buttons," said Stephen. "I got the usual bullshit from the man I shared it with, but I'd been warned and I just took it with a clerical sweetness."

"I suspect you're getting the soap bug," said Philip.

"I think I might be, just for a year or two."

"Wouldn't even a year as a well-meaning clergyman be a bit limiting?"

"Oh, I wasn't thinking necessarily of *Jubilee Terrace*," said Stephen, obviously trying not to sound cocky. "I've got three weeks' work on *Emmerdale* coming up when I sign off here."

"Good Lord!" said Philip, genuinely impressed. "Jobs on two soaps and you haven't even finished drama school!"

The young man's cherubic face assumed a deprecatory expression.

"Oh, it was luck. You were there in the church, weren't you? And I heard that *Emmerdale* was looking for a young Australian. Pure good fortune."

Philip Marston gaped.

"You're not Australian, are you? I heard nothing—"

"I'm as Aussie as they come, Cobber. Watch your mouth when you mention God's own country or I'll land one on you that you won't forget in a hurry."

Philip Marston pondered.

"When people say they're as Aussie as they come I usually find their people went out there when he or she was two or three. Oh and, by the bye, you haven't got the regulation tan either."

Stephen Barrymore looked shamefaced.

"Actually, that is what happened to me. As to the tan, you must have heard the word 'pommies.' Most of the English who emigrate go red in the Australian sun, or pink like a pomegranate. I'm surprised you didn't hear any Australian in the accent, though."

"Lots of Australians are very good at English pronunciation, but they usually slip up on something or other: 'salt,' for example, or 'school.'"

"Oh, I can say 'sawlt' with the best of you English. But if it comes up in the *Emmerdale* scripts I'll rhyme it with 'colt.' At home we always pronounced in the English way. My parents have never adapted. They'd die rather than spend Christmas Day on the beach. My mother has sleepless nights when someone mistakes her for an Aussie."

"So when are you recording *Emmerdale*?"

"A month's time."

"And who are you playing?"

"Louise's kid brother. Come over to see all the people she's mentioned, which means mostly the people she has slept with. Chance to bring him back again later on—once he's been around and taken his fill of the Old Country."

"Well, well: doors are opening for you."

The same idea had occurred to Marjorie Harcourt-Smith. She had left her table near the bar and nipped across to where Reggie was standing, near the door to the Terrace. Marjorie had a surprising turn of speed when she was after something.

"I don't think you can have heard that, Reggie—"

Reggie sighed.

"Get to the point, Marjorie. We're busy."

"The new curate, Stephen Barrymore: he's got a bit part in *Emmerdale*. Starts when he finishes with us, playing Louise's brother from Australia. He is Australian, though he's been keeping it quiet. There's already talk in the *Emmerdale* camp of using him again later in the year."

She was delighted to see she had caught Reggie's attention at once.

"Really? The snakes! Jumping in like that."

"Reggie, *please* could he come and lodge with me? It would be ideal."

"Marjorie, I'm surprised at you. At your age. And I happen to know you've only one bedroom."

"Don't be silly, Reggie. I mean on the Terrace. Gladys Porter desperately needs someone to react to, someone of the opposite sex to talk things over with, have special little scenes with."

"You rat, Marjorie." The voice was Winnie's, from behind her left ear. "Jumping the gun like that. Reggie, if he is to lodge anywhere on the Terrace it should definitely be with me. With Lady Wharton. We formed a close bond during the terrible time he was visiting the dying Cyril. He's become quite a second son to her. And a good deal nicer than the first one."

Marjorie turned, rather condescendingly, to her.

"Winnie, darling, you're being quite unreasonable. You

were on your own all the time Cyril was in San Francisco or wherever it was. And it suited you. As a *lady* you feel alone in the Terrace. But I've only just lost Vernon—Bert, I mean—and I'm finding it very difficult. It would be natural for Gladys to offer Stephen her spare room. I've been talking to Melvin about Gladys's need, and I'm sure he'll back me up."

"I've heard he was thinking of bringing on someone you've met at the University of the Third Age," said Reggie mischievously. "There's any number of more or less male would-be actors who'd give their right arms to play him. Now go away and squabble elsewhere. I'll think this over when I've got this scene in the can."

Philip Marston, who by now was sitting at a table by the window with his *Terrace* wife, Carol Chisholm, had watched this exchange with a cynical smile on his face (an expression that was never allowed to cross it when shooting *Terrace,* for which he had a small repertoire of dependable and concerned expressions). He said to Carol, "Marjorie and Winnie are both bearding Reggie. I bet I know what they're after."

"What's that?"

"*Who,* more like. They've heard that this new curate has got an in-and-out job on *Emmerdale,* and they want Reggie to step in now and offer him a six-month contract, probably with an option of a further six."

"Why should they care?"

"They want to be his landlady on the Terrace. They both lack a regular partner—in the widest sense—who they can build a relationship with, have sparring matches with, or just humorous exchanges. They think young

Stephen seems eminently likeable, and they both covet him."

"Likeable actors frequently turn out to be anything but underneath the veneer. Anyway, we can acquit them of lust. He is not exactly a sex bombshell . . . Still, he might add something to the Kerridge household. Be a replacement for the son in the Merchant Navy."

"You forget we've only got two bedrooms. Both taken."

"Can't we get rid of that bitch Dawn? Isn't she just the type to go to university? Nobody does in soaps, and a woman doing it might even be a first. I think Ken Barlow was the last to go in *Corrie,* and that must have been in the early sixties. But in real life everybody's going, and studying all sorts of quite outlandish subjects. Dawn could go and study the History and Social Significance of Cosmetic Surgery, and this Stephen could have her room."

"That's no go."

"Why not?"

"She'd never leave Leeds, wouldn't Dawn."

"Why not?"

"Because our Susan would be years before she could get another job that paid as well, and gives her national exposure."

"That's not in Susan's hands."

"She'd use every weapon, and Susan has many weapons, including a high degree of adhesiveness."

"That's the only one of her weapons she never uses on Bill Garrett. Every muscle in her body says *noli me tangere.*"

They giggled—close, almost like real married people.

They watched as Bill slipped from behind the bar and went over to Susan Fyldes's table. He stopped by it, obviously wondering whether he could sit companionably on it, then did exactly that. Susan leaned back in her chair, clearly unenchanted by Bill's hindquarters.

"Good that you can come into the Duke of York's at last," he said. Susan removed the plugs and wires from her ears with palpable reluctance.

"What?" she asked. It was not the yobbish teenager's "What?" but a middle-class matron's "What?" addressed to a social inferior not eligible for "I beg your pardon."

"I said it's good you can come into the Duke of York's at last," repeated Bill, his heart already sinking.

"You know I've been going into pubs for years," said Susan.

"But that was Susan. I'm just saying I'm glad that Dawn has caught up with Susan, and I can expect scenes with her."

Susan rummaged in her handbag and took out her mobile phone.

"Do you mind—I'm busy. I've got to ring my mother— my real mother, who gave birth to me, not my soap mother. That shouldn't have to be explained every time my mother's mentioned, but apparently it has to be. You're old, Bill. You're played out. You're a nothing guy, so in future, Bill, will you please stop wasting my time, because I certainly won't be wasting yours."

"Fuck you, madam," was Bill's comment, but only in his mind.

"Have you noticed," he said to Liza Croome, his soap wife when he was back behind the bar, drawing his forearm across his forehead, and looking at Garry Kopps and Shirley Merritt, who were seated on stools on the public's side of the bar, "that the English have become incapable of communicating with each other? They plug crap music into their ears to prevent encounters of any sort. They don't want to talk to people face-to-face, they don't even want to talk to them by phone, so they do it by mobile, where you've got a rotten line that robs the voice of any individuality and frequently fades entirely. They advertise free mobile calls under the slogan 'Widen your social circle.' Nobody cooks, they just watch cookery programs. They live out a surrogate life through television, watching setup situations, which they laughingly call 'reality TV' and then they—"

"Bill," said Garry Kopps.

"Yes?"

"She slapped you down, didn't she?"

"Yes. Told me to get lost. Said I was a nothing guy."

"And you knew perfectly well, didn't you, that that would be the result, made more likely by your planting your fat arse on her table?"

"Well, I wasn't expecting her to throw her arms around me."

"Why can't you ever learn?" said Liza. "That's what Garry is trying to say."

"Because I don't want to, Liza, I suppose. I'm not that old. If only she'd—"

But at that point Reggie bellowed out a call for action, and everyone took their allotted instead of their chosen places. The filming of the scenes went ahead with the rather unexciting efficiency that long familiarity with characters and settings inevitably produces. During the session the camera jumped from group to group in the old-fashioned bar: over by the window the Kerridges were joined by Gladys Porter, and the three of them discussed the latter's loneliness and the progress of Dawn's romance with James. The question of James's color did not come up, and neither did the question of whether they had slept together. The second of these subjects would come up, but the first never would. Meanwhile Dawn was filmed on her mobile, talking not to her mother but to James, with whom she had some sub-Juliet love talk.

Over the beer pumps the Bradleys from the corner shop moaned to the Worseleys, the only bar staff on that night, about the difficulty of getting and keeping casual workers. They went together well, being all in the service-with-a-social-conscience line. Meanwhile Lady Wharton, alone as Gladys had proclaimed her to be, drank her gin and tonic in a dignified and benign manner.

When the scenes in their scripts had been filmed, Reggie held up his hand for silence.

"There's just one more scene. Just a couple of minutes. Here, Stephen, Winnie—read this over and tell me if you could have a conversation roughly along these lines."

Winnie looked terrified for a moment, then reluctantly removed her spectacles from her handbag. Stephen came from his snug position over near the darts board and took the page with a confidence that, if only apparent, was at least convincing.

"I think we could do that, don't you, Winnie?" he said, without a break in his voice. Winnie looked up anxiously at the producer.

"Let me get this right, Reggie. You want us to have a few words, which we make up ourselves, about the state of Cyril's mind and likely death in the next few days?"

"That's right."

"Nothing on paper, and we just make up something appropriate?"

"Exactly."

"Well, I suppose we can try."

Reggie sent Stephen over to the main door, and the cameras rolled. Stephen went outside, then opened the door, looking nervously from end to end of the public bar, the quintessential unsure-of-himself cleric in a strange pub. He finally saw Winnie on her own at a small table, and walked over to her with more confidence.

"Do you mind if I join you, Lady Wharton?"

"Not at all. I'd be delighted. Beer? A pint of Thornberrys, Bob."

The curate waited until the beer was in front of him before he said, "I'm sure I don't have to tell you, Lady Wharton, that Cyril is quite a bit worse than when I saw him the last time."

Winnie shook her head miserably, with a strangled "No."

"I don't expect you to feel as strongly as I do about his mental state—"

"You mean his spiritual state, don't you?"

"Yes. My hope is that he might come to terms with God and his approaching death before he is beyond thought."

Lady Wharton pursed her lips.

"I'm an Anglican myself, of course, but Cyril has never

been interested. And no—I can't say that's much in my mind, his spiritual state. I've faced up to what is going to happen, and what I want is for him to have as easy a death as possible."

"Believe it or not that is what I want too."

Stephen leaned forward in order to discuss matters of faith when *"Cut!"* called Reggie from the door. He came down to the center of the Duke of York's set. "That was perfect. Just what I wanted: both of you entirely natural and convincing. It went much better than most scripts. We must think over what that means for the scripts generally. Right—that's it for tonight." He looked at his watch. "I'm sorry for the evening shoot, but it was the only way we could fit it in. Sleep well, my children, or whatever else you choose to do."

The actors began a brisk exodus from the set, aiming in the direction of the Northern TV building's main exit. Bill and Liza dallied behind the bar, as if there was unfinished business they wanted to talk over. Finally Bill said, "You got half an hour or so, Liza?"

"You know I always have for you, Bill."

"Come on, then. Let's go and find a pub."

The figure came out of the front door of the house illuminated only by a dim light from the hall, which immediately shut off. It slipped to the side of the house and picked up something from just inside the open garage. The hood of its anorak was pulled over the face, and its right hand now carried not only a can of some kind, but also some tightly folded paper. It scuttled to the gate and headed in the direction of the city center, pulling now and then at the hood and keeping its head well down, as if studying the configuration of the pavement.

The walk was not a long one, perhaps twenty minutes, but it stopped short of Leeds—slowing down as it neared the area with a view toward the West Yorkshire Playhouse. The streets here were mean, but mean these days meant affordable, and individuals or organizations that had bought up some of them made sterling efforts to clean the brickwork, install bigger windows, freshen the outer paintwork. Cheerful, brightly lit, dashingly papered interiors could be seen through some of the windows. The figure stopped some way from its goal, cautiously pushing the hood back a mite, gazing intently.

There was a light on in the targeted house, one of a terrace of attached houses. But there was only one light, upstairs. Perhaps it was in one of the bedrooms. The figure put its twin burdens down by the wall of a disused factory, and hid them as well as possible by standing near them. Twenty minutes later the light in the terraced house went out. The figure did not stir.

It was a quarter of an hour later, during which all had been quiet in the house, when the shape suddenly reached into its left-hand pocket and took out something, then into the right-hand pocket and did the same. Two minutes later it replaced them, then looked toward the house, number nine. It was in darkness. The figure bent to pick up paper and can, and moved cautiously forward. Standing for a moment outside the front door the observer (if there had been one) might have seen that the paper was a tabloid—maybe the *Sun,* maybe the *Times*—

whose pages had first been torn apart, then torn in half. Several of the pages were soaked from the can, then pushed through the door. Finally one of the sheets was folded up as a spill, lit with a cigarette lighter, then stuffed hurriedly through the door.

As the flame lit up the open letterbox the figure hared off down the street in the direction it had come, leaving the can behind to add to the conflagration when the door collapsed. It had been a very thorough job, a credit to the planning that had gone into it. It did what it was intended it should do.

The pub that Bill and Liza found was the Red Deer, just off Upper Briggate, in the center of Leeds. In its brasswork, its faded sepia photographs, and its heavy wood tables and settles, it was not unlike the Duke of York's on the *Jubilee* set, which may have been its attraction to Bill and Liza. Bill looked around contentedly.

"Makes me feel at home, this place," he said. Liza laughed.

"You always say that. But the Duke of York's is not your home."

"It's as much a home as I've had since my childhood one. The girls are the only things that give the present one any feeling of home. God forgive me for never giving them a real one."

"You've given them quite as good a home as most kids have these days," said Liza loyally. Bill stirred uneasily in his chair.

"Well, Angela and I have done what we could, and not done bad. But it's not fair on Angela, is it? She's forced to be old before her time . . . One good thing, though: at least I'm cured of that snotty little bitch Susan Fyldes."

"That wasn't what you said back at the Duke of York's, after she'd given you a right squashing, as far as I could see."

"I've thought it over since. It's the best thing that could have happened. Fine thing it would have been, wouldn't it, if I'd introduced her into the family, she only five or six years older than my Angela. Not to mention that she's no more motherly than the bitch I'm married to now."

"So what makes you think you're over her?" asked Liza carefully. Bill didn't respond well to skepticism about his resolutions.

"I was getting over it already. Really I was. Then tonight she told me to get out of her space, said I was a nothing man. It wasn't just the words, it was the tone of voice, the expression on her face. Reminded me of Bet."

"Well, that's a relief, I admit. Now at least you can go forward. Concentrate on getting custody of the children in the divorce."

Bill bent forward over the table, his face red with anger.

"Custody shouldn't even be an issue! Bet's never been interested in the girls—they've always been a burden to her, nothing more than that. Her application for custody must be pure mischief. Or someone else is putting her up to it."

"Who would?" asked Liza thoughtfully. Then she said, "Of course, there is Hamish Fawley."

"Her supposed fiancé. But why would he? I've never done him any harm."

"I don't suppose Stephen Barrymore has either, but it doesn't stop Hamish being poisonous to him."

Bill shifted uneasily again, an agonized expression on his face.

"Unless he's serious about the marriage, and wants . . . wants to get control of three young girls."

It was out—the nightmare from the back of his brain.

"But why would he? The fact that he's bedding Bet doesn't suggest he's the type who's attracted by school-girls."

Bill just shook his head.

"The attraction may not be sex so much as . . . tormenting them, torturing them by pressing sex on them—sex with someone they fear and hate."

It was Liza's turn to shake her head.

"Well, all I can say is I've never heard that perversion alleged of Hamish, and I've heard practically every activity on God's earth attributed to him at one time or another. Snap out of it, Bill, or it will affect the girls."

"Yes, yes," muttered Bill. He shook himself. "It was just worst-case scenario imaginings. And really the girls are fine, not upset because their mother's gone. The worst thing that could happen is they'll have a rotten diet. Angela has grown up thinking food means takeaways. And she and I will stop that if the younger ones start putting on weight."

"Of course you will. You will come through this, and with flying colors. I know you will."

Liza was experienced in conversations with Bill, and was adept at hiding any reservations she might feel. She knew him so well. When he said, "I've got to go to the loo," she knew he was going to ring his three daughters. They were the only important women in his life.

The figure scurried through the near-deserted streets, confidently negotiating the winding and intersecting highways as if it were the keeper of a maze. The anorak was clutched around its body and the bottom of the jeans were getting dusty from the ill-swept roads. The hood was kept pulled down over head and face, which continued to look intently at the road. Because, behind it, now several yards away, a red glow in the sky suggested a fire. And in the distance sirens started, coming nearer and fast. But in the end the figure knew they would arrive too late. One of the firemen expressed on television the same fatalism the next day.

"There was nothing anybody could do," he said.

CHAPTER 7

A Burned-Out Case

✳

Surveying the scene the next morning, in the chilly and grimy light of day, Charlie Peace was struck by the meanness of it all. The house where Hamish Fawley died was new and spruce, yet the skimped space for all the activities of life made it seem mean—a mean house, in a mean little street, in a mean area of Leeds, with the hideous modern palace of the Department of Work and Pensions within all-too-easy walking distance. All this, and then the burned entrance area, with burned door and window frames, evidences of a hatred, or a fear, or a contempt that condemned a man and a woman to a hideous death—all seemed to add up to a sadly appropriate end to Hamish Fawley, in tune with the meanness of spirit of the man, as Charlie had seen it in action in the studios of Northern Television.

Charlie had been called at home in Slepton Edge and sent to an address in Leeds, where his least favorite policeman, Superintendent Birnley, was waiting for him.

Waiting, he had no doubt, to off-load on him the grind of the investigation, while retaining for himself all the glory of publicity that could be milked from the very public nature of the victims. With a sigh that developed into a groan Charlie donned his white protective clothing, and went into the blackened and smoke-smelling hallway, then upstairs to the bedroom. Birnley acknowledged his arrival with a grunt, then resumed his random survey of the charred room, in particular the two bodies—one half on and half off the bed, the other over by the window.

"Right," said Birnley finally. "I've got to go back to HQ. There's going to be a lot of public interest in this: second-highest-ranking soap in the ratings, behind *Coronation Street*, of course, but way ahead of *EastEnders*. What have we got here that I can tell a press conference? I don't think there's any doubt it's a bloke called Hamish Fawley, who was renting this little love nest from Northern Television. The woman is his fiancée, Bet Garrett, also currently in *Jubilee Terrace*. I've had a few words with the producer, Reggie Friedman, and I'll wise up with someone who watches the program and try and sound as if I did when I talk to the media."

Charlie had also been surveying the room.

"I phoned the casting people at NTV on the way here," Charlie said. "Just to get a few basic facts. Bet Garrett, the fiancée, is the estranged wife of the man who plays Bob Worseley in *Terrace*. He's a middle-aged man, and these clothes don't suggest they'd be worn by a woman his wife's age."

He gestured to a chair in the corner of the bedroom,

only mildly singed, on which lay a very skimpy skirt decorated around the waist (or groin) with chains, beads, and buckles. Birnley favored him with an elaborate sigh.

"Laddie"—Charlie particularly disliked his habit of calling him that, Birnley not having a drop of Scottish blood in his veins—"have you never heard of mutton dressed up as lamb? Or for that matter, have you never watched a middle-aged man making a fool of himself, even unto marriage, with much younger meat?"

"The Garretts have teenaged children so Bet Garrett couldn't be too young."

"Well, you'll find it's her, all the same. Friedman was pretty sure about the engagement."

Charlie felt he need do no more to enjoin caution on his superior. It ought to be the other way around, he thought.

"Well, I'll be on my way," said Birnley, picking up his papers. "I could easily walk to police headquarters from here if I was that way inclined." He smirked around the little group. "Very considerate of our murderer."

"Are we quite sure it was murder?" asked Charlie.

"Oh, no doubt in the world. Didn't you smell the petrol? Pretty funny way to commit suicide, eh?"

Charlie thought he could be in for a right rollicking if he recommended caution on two fronts. Anyway, he felt pretty sure that on this matter Birnley was right. He had not often met a more murderable victim than Hamish Fawley.

"What did Reggie say? What did you learn?"

The cast of *Jubilee Terrace* were scattered around the

canteen with but a single thought in their heads. Les Crosby, who played Harry Hornby the newsagent, had been seen talking to Reggie as they went up the steps of the Northern Television studios, and the two had gone together to Reggie's office. That was enough to make the actors shout their questions to Les. He turned and came over.

"What are you talking about? I didn't *learn* anything. There is a new plotline for Young Foulmouth—a strike of newspaper boys and girls. Reggie wanted to be sure I was happy about the way things were being planned, and we got on to possible consequences later on: maybe one of the newspaper girls becoming a sort of surrogate daughter for Lady Wharton."

"But what did he say about Hamish?"

Les Crosby frowned in bewilderment.

"Why should he say anything about Hamish? We don't all need to discuss him morning, noon, and night, you know. As a matter of fact he didn't mention him."

"In other words, you haven't heard," put in Garry Kopps.

"Haven't heard what?"

"Hamish has died in a fire in his house," said Shirley Merritt, who played Maureen Bradley of the corner shop. "Bet Garrett died as well."

"Good God." Les Crosby sat down, and started drinking someone else's coffee. "How did the fire start? And where was this house where Hamish was living?"

"Hallway we heard," said Garry Kopps. "And in one of those NTV houses not far from the West Yorkshire Playhouse."

"You're thinking what the rest of us are thinking," said Winnie Hey to Les.

"Probably. But remember Vernon. We all thought someone had pushed him in front of a bus when we heard about his accident."

"Not all of us—only some. And who's to say we were wrong?" said Carol Chisholm.

"Point taken. I wasn't around when that copper came sniffing. But one anonymous letter doesn't make a murder case."

"Nobody said it did," said Philip Marston calmly. "I think we should put a bung into speculation like that. Say someone put petrol and a lighted match through the letterbox and so killed Hamish and Bet. They're the most hated members of the cast. Who's going to be the first to come under suspicion?"

They thought about this.

"I didn't hate Bet Garrett," said Marjorie. "I hardly knew her."

"Exactly," said Philip. "*Because* you hardly knew her you didn't hate her . . . Actually a lot of us loathed her for what she was doing to Bill and the children."

"We only have Bill's word for most of that," said Garry Kopps.

"But we believe it because Bill is the straightest of us all, and the moralist in the Terrace. He's a good man, and Bet was a cheap tart."

"You're committing the vulgar error that all fans make, of confusing the actor and the part he plays," went on Garry Kopps. "Bill is a moralist and a model to us all when he is playing Bob Worseley—the man who can keep order in a public bar and shame any man—or woman—who steps out of line. But I wouldn't give tuppence for any morality or judgment that issued from the mouth of Bill Garrett. Look at the kind of woman he married, for a start."

"It's because of all he's suffered and learned while he was married to Bet that I'd accept what he said as moral guidance," said Philip Marston.

Several of the cast nodded: they'd listen to, if not necessarily follow, moral guidance from good old Bill. No one analyzed their reactions to the man. If they had, they would have realized that they were really unsure where Bob Worseley ended and Bill Garrett began. And the same ambivalence, though he showed no awareness of the fact, was true of Garry Kopps. He played a similar role as moral arbiter in the corner shop, where people gathered. And other cast members often talked about him as if he *were* Arthur Bradley, and ought to be given a five-minute God-slot on Radio Four.

Charlie Peace, alone in the bedroom of the charred house, stood and looked around the last resting place of the charred corpse he assumed was Hamish Fawley. He hated murder scenes, but had got used to suppressing his nausea. They were a regular but not a frequent part of his job. He preferred other sorts of cases that required from him pretty much what a murder case (other than a crime of passion) did: insight into ingenuity and ambiguity; psychological perception: ability to sort out the relevant from the merely incidental.

He crossed to the upright chair under the window.

Hamish's jeans and shirt were under the women's clothes that he had noticed before, and also a handbag. He looked into that first, his hands protected by the latex gloves. He always thought he looked like a down-market chef in his protective gear. The handbag turned out to be the nearest thing to a makeup case. Nothing of interest. He put his hand into the tight pocket in the front of the ridiculous shirt. There was a card there. Gingerly he pulled it out. It was an Equity card—that prized permission-to-act for all would-be professional performers. Only this one was in the name of Sylvia Cardew. A tentatively smiling teenage face grinned out from the card. Charlie whistled.

He went through in his mind all the possibilities: that Bet Garrett acted under a stage name, or possibly her maiden one, and this was an old picture of her. Whence "Bet," though? That Bet had had a marriage earlier than the one to Bill, and this was her first married name, and a photograph that flattered her and concealed her age.

But somehow, from the little Charlie knew of Hamish from his brief encounter with the *Jubilee* cast, the alternative explanation seemed to be the most likely one: that Hamish was playing away from his fiancée, that this was indeed a genuine and recent picture of the woman whose burned body still lay on the bed, and that she was a teenager, or a not-long-since teenager as the photograph suggested—naive, keen to get ahead in the acting profession, and willing to do anything to ensure that. Sad.

"If you want to get ahead, go to bed," he said, adapting an old advertising slogan. He took his mobile from his pocket.

"Rani? It's Charlie Peace. I need to get a message through to Superintendent Birnley. As quick as you can. I believe he's going to hold a press conference about now."

"He is. Pretty premature, I'd say."

"Yes, well, there's no holding an old trouper back. The message is that I've found in the clothing of the woman found in Hamish Fawley's bed an Equity card with the name Sylvia Cardew on it. He needs to keep stum and not give any name to the female victim—OK?"

"OK. I've got a minute or two before the press conference opens. Enjoy yourself, Charlie."

Detective Constable Omkar Rani went straight to the pressroom, which was already crowded and stuffy. No policemen at the top table. He went and stood outside. Within seconds he saw at the end of a long corridor the figure of Superintendent Birnley: his walk showed intense enjoyment of the approaching publicity, the set of his shoulders suggested he was about to announce the winning of a war. As he came nearer the expression of intense self-satisfaction on his face became nauseatingly apparent to DC Rani, who stepped forward, proffering the paper with Charlie's message on it.

"Sir, I have an important message from Inspector Peace, which he thinks—"

Birnley snatched the paper, gave an almost imperceptible nod, and marched ahead into the pressroom. Rani, looking through the still-open door, saw him shoving the message into his trouser pocket.

Oh well, stuff you, he thought, and marched away,

determined to let him stew. Too few of his underlings had done this in the course of Superintendent Birnley's less-than-shining police career.

The set for the back rooms of the Duke of York's was one that few of the soap's actors saw in the course of filming. These rooms were usually sacred to the Worseleys (Bill Garrett and Liza Croome), the bar staff, and occasionally the bar staff's emotional entanglements of the moment.

Today all the currently-being-filmed staff were crowded into them. There was still only one topic of conversation: the death of Hamish and Bet Garrett. It was spoken of as murder, and hardly anyone doubted for a moment that that was what it was. There were slightly different verdicts on each corpse, however.

"There's no doubt whatever that Hamish asked for it," said Carol Chisholm, her voice halfway between its natural tones and those of Norma Kerridge. "He tried to insult and diminish everyone involved in the show."

"Except maybe Reggie," put in Philip Marston, her *Terrace* husband.

"He was dependent on Reggie for employment," said Carol. "However much he stressed he was slumming it, it was work, and a good regular wage. Have you heard of offers to him from the National or the Royal Shake-speare? And we would have . . . But Bet I don't feel so sure about. I didn't know her at all well. OK, she'd married unwisely, and she led Bill a merry dance and invited in anyone who looked in her direction, including more than one who's here now." She looked around, and met only glances of wide-eyed innocence, a well-practiced expression. "But to a greater or lesser degree most of us here have been there, done that."

"Speak for yourself," said Marjorie. "My husband and I split up because we were fed up with each other. I hated everything he did, his gestures, his expressions, his opinions. And yet in a way we are still good friends. After all, everyone has friends who bore or irritate them. And I certainly never led him a merry dance, whatever that implies."

"The thing about Bet," said Les Crosby, "was that she was totally and entirely for herself, and that was allied with a peculiar and usually sadistic sense of humor."

They considered this.

"Sounds the ideal mate for Hamish Fawley," said Garry Kopps. "They could torment each other."

"You do realize she was supposed to be filming today, don't you?" said Marjorie. "Another flower-shop scene, for after Cyril's death. I suppose they could just use anyone, as one of whatever-her-name-is's assistants."

"Rita Somerville, that's what her name is," said Philip Marston. "Oh—here's Stephen. I think he's been talking to Reggie. Oh God—look. He's got Young Foulmouth with him."

Young Foulmouth had a baptismal name that hardly anyone knew or could remember. In fact it was Theodor Mossby. In the *Terrace* he played the only child of Bill Garrett and his *Terrace* wife, Liza Croome. His soap name was Jason, and his antics, cheek, and elaborate tricks filled many a vacant five minutes of *Terrace* time. His unlovely countertenor voice (he was fourteen but playing twelve, and was adept at masking the effects of a broken voice) floated across the studio to them.

"'Course I'm not worried about a cunt like him who's dead. That's what you get if you fuck around like he did. You get jealous husbands or lovers watching your back, waiting for you to leave off your bulletproof vest—it's fucking natural, innit?"

"Hamish Fawley wasn't shot," said Stephen.

"I didn't say he was, cloth-head," said Young Foulmouth. "I just said someone would be after him. He had his eyes on a new one yesterday. Fucking gorgeous she was too. I thought I could pop in there and show her how it's done. She'd be grateful for a good fuck from someone who knows the way after a fucking geriatric like Fawley had been on her. I don't suppose he'd had time to get her to bed yesterday, though." He put on a terrible parody of Eartha Kitt's voice. "An Englishman needs *time*."

"Stephen," came the most-upper-crust-attainable voice of Winnie Hey.

"Yes, Winnie?"

"You know, when there's swearing on TV before the watershed time for programming with adult material, they put this funny *phut* sound instead?"

"Yes."

"Couldn't you manage the same sort of effect with Young Foulmouth here by shoving one of those rubber plunger things they use to unblock drains down his throat every time you expect an offense against decency?"

"I could give it a try, Winnie. I'd have to run it past Reggie first."

"You keep your fucking plunger thing to yourself," said Theodor. But he made a strategic retreat to a far corner of the studio, and stood nursing his dignity.

Everyone was looking at Stephen.

"Who was this girl that Hamish had his eye on yester-day?" Phil Marston asked.

"Search me."

"Reggie didn't mention it?" asked Winnie.

"No. Why should he? I'm only concerned with Hamish as Cyril, and I won't be that for much longer. Reggie just wanted to say how good the death scene had been in what was supposed to be a run-through. He says he can use it all, and fake anything else he needs. If he wants more stuff with the hands on the bedclothes he can use any old hands—almost. He said we could have an audition for look-alike hands."

"Anybody here in filming yesterday?" asked Philip, looking around.

"There was the evening filming, of course," said Marjorie. "Most of us were there. Earlier there was a big scene between the Worseleys, worried their mischievous offspring was getting out of hand. I was in the pub, but most of the scene took place in here, the private quarters. But I think there must have been a flower-shop scene. I saw Bet Garrett hanging around in her shop overall. Was that why you were in, Les?"

"Yes. I was in the shop buying flowers for Cyril's funeral."

It occurred to all of them that Les had been rather backward in coming forward, but it occurred to none of them to mention it. They were all playing down any connections they had with Bet or Hamish.

"Was there anyone else in the scene, anyone new? Another customer, maybe?"

"No, but there was a new girl in the shop, learning to make up wreaths and bouquets. Pretty little thing."

"But why would Hamish be there? Young Foulmouth saw him. Cyril is dead by then."

"He could have been there to keep his eye on Bet. Though he was the one who most needed watching over."

"Oh, come off it, do," said Marjorie impatiently. "They weren't *watching* each other. That engagement was nothing but a con. They weren't 'in love,' whatever that may mean. It was just a means of aggravating Bill."

"And perhaps the daughters too," put in Winnie. "I wouldn't put that past Bet. Not aggravating them, but really worrying them."

"But nothing you've said explains what Hamish's motives were," said Carol Chisholm. "Why did he help Bet get a rise out of Bill? Hamish didn't go around doing good turns. He wasn't a born-again Boy Scout. Why did he go along with it, Garry?"

"Sheer mischief," he said. One of Garry Kopps's claims to be the *Terrace's* intellectual was a two-year course in psychology. "Devilry. Delight in causing *angst*."

"He just likes fucking people up, you mean," said Young Foulmouth, who had edged his way back into the discussion.

"Something like that," agreed Les Crosby.

But the discussion got no further. Everyone suddenly went silent. From the corridor came the vicious clank of heels that one would have thought were made out of iron castings. Some of those waiting in silence thought they had heard those shoes before, others had pictures in their minds of wedge heels and gold lamé straps.

The door pushed open.

"What the hell is going on here?" demanded Bet Garrett. "Why is everybody looking at me as if I've just returned from the dead?"

"Because you just have, ducky," said Garry Kopps.

CHAPTER 8

Actors Born and Made

✳

There was a dreadful hush for a few seconds, then Marjorie Harcourt-Smith took pity on the new arrival, who was by now looking from face to face.

"Bet, there's no way of telling you this gently. I'm afraid Hamish has died in a fire at the house he was renting. Someone else died with him, and we thought—and I think the police thought—it must be you."

No one had expected anguished sobbing, since Bet had probably been using Hamish for plans of her own, but they had not expected total cool. Total cool, however, was what they got.

"Hamish, eh? Well, I suppose he asked for it."

"Is that all you've got to say?" demanded Winnie, as if she had loved Hamish like a mother.

"Pretty much," said Bet, undaunted. "We'd more or less split up days ago, though we'd decided not to say anything about it."

"So Bill wouldn't know?" asked Philip Marston, as cool as she was.

"Draw your own bloody conclusions," said Bet. "Well, I don't think that this affects me in any way. I've got a scene with you, Carol, haven't I? I'll be getting along to Makeup—see you later."

She started off toward the door, but was struck by a thought and turned around.

"You said someone else was killed. You can see it wasn't me. You can touch me if you like—it wouldn't be the first time for some of you. So who was the other body?"

"We don't really know—" began Stephen.

"Why the embarrassment? Was she a bed partner?"

"It seems likely. As Marjorie said, the fire was at the house Hamish was renting from Northern TV. We doubt he was showing the lady his etchings."

"Well, go on. Who was it?"

"We don't know," said Winnie. "Not *know*. You have to be careful after a mistake has been made, and we think even the police had decided it was you. But there is an idea—it came from Young Foulmouth, actually—that Hamish had his eye on a young person in the flower shop."

Bet raised her eyebrows.

"Oh *her*. What was her name now? I can't remember. But Hamish was hanging around the set yesterday. I thought at first he was trying to make things up with me, but beyond a casual greeting he was obviously more interested in the apprentice florist rather than the old hand."

She was surprised when a dark face over a natty suit appeared from the shadows of the doorway.

"Was the name Sylvia Cardew?" asked Charlie Peace.

"That's it! Bloody boring name if you ask me." Bet's face twisted into a grin. "Well, that's another young career shot down in flames before it even got off the ground. I'm off to Makeup." She raised her hand. *"Ciao."*

"Wait!" said Charlie, catching her by the arm. "Can you confirm that you are Bet Garrett?"

"Yes. 'Course I bloody can."

She looked around the set, and Charlie's eyes followed hers. All of the cast members assembled there without exception nodded. Bet scurried away, and Charlie retreated to a far part of the large set and took out his mobile phone. He tried Rani but there was no response. He dialed another number.

"Cathy? It's Charlie Peace here. Is the chief super available? . . . Damn. Could you get a message to him? . . . Right: 'From DI Peace. I have just seen and spoken to Bet Garrett. If her name has not so far come up in our dealings with the press—'"

"It has," came Cathy's voice.

"Double damn. But leave it as it is . . . 'dealings with the press. Something needs to be done fast.' That's about it. Could you rephrase it so it doesn't sound as if I'm teaching the chief super his job?"

"He's used to that from you, Charlie, but I'll try."

Charlie put his phone away and turned back to the cast.

"Now, this is what used to be called a turn-up for the book. Or you might say we've fallen—the police have—flat on our faces. All the assumptions we've made have been turned upside down."

"Why did you make them, then?" asked Garry Kopps. They were made, Charlie thought, by an ass called Birnley after a talk with Reggie Friedman. He lodged that thought in the back of his brain but did not give it voice.

"Hamish Fawley and Bet Garrett have been engaged for how long?" he asked. Philip Marston shrugged and replied.

"About three weeks."

"And disengaged for how long?"

"You probably heard her say 'days ago.'"

"Anybody have any independent confirmation of this, and how long ago it happened?"

No voice spoke up. Heads were shaken.

"Am I right in thinking there was a general skepticism about this engagement? Whether it was made in earnest, and whether it was ever likely to lead to a marriage?"

This time Marjorie replied.

"No one could see Bet jumping straight from one disastrous marriage into another. And no one could imagine Hamish getting married at all."

Charlie thought.

"So there is no reason to assume that a big row led to the breakup of the engagement. They could just have decided that the joke had gone on long enough."

"Definitely," said Philip. "I don't think any of us here heard of any row, but as you say there didn't need to be one."

"So who was this joke engagement, if that's what it was, aimed at? What was the point?"

"It was to drive poor old Bill mental," said Les Crosby.

"Most of what Bet has done in the last few years has been aimed at that. The centerpiece to the recent stuff has been Bet's demand for custody of the three girls."

"Why would that be a surprise?" asked Charlie. "The mother is usually given custody."

"If she wants it. Bet was the archetypal negligent mother. Bill had always assumed that the custody would be awarded him by default."

Charlie had a distinct impression that some cast members were trying to hush Les Crosby, but couldn't pin down who.

"Let's get this straight. Bill Garrett was convinced that his wife's attempt to get custody was a serious one, even if her motive was just to spite him."

He looked around. There were several reluctant nods.

"And Bill Garrett gave no sign that he knew the engagement had been called off—if it was ever on?"

"None of us knew, so far as I'm aware," said Philip Marston. "We all heard of the breakup for the first time five minutes ago, when you did."

"Interesting," said Charlie. He sensed all eyes on him, but said nothing about why he found it interesting. His mind was building up a house of cards in which Bill Garrett came to the conclusion that the move for custody came more from Hamish than from Bet, and that what Hamish had his eyes on was three very attractive girls, all under sixteen. If this was so, a lot could depend on whether Bill had heard of the end of the engagement, in which case Hamish would become much less interesting to him. On the other hand, if the engagement was still on so far as Bill was concerned, the wiping out of Hamish made good sense, and the assumption that Bet would be included in the package made murder at the very least a possibility, almost a likelihood.

"What time was the fire?"

The voice came from over by the door. Charlie looked around and saw a female face that he recognized.

"I'm sorry, I forget your name. Maybe you didn't give it to me when we met last time."

"Liza Croome. Married *Terrace*-wise to Bob Worseley, the landlord of the Duke of York's—that's Bill Garrett. I asked what time the fire was."

"Yes, I heard you. A neighbor called emergency at nine thirty-two last night."

Liza did not need to think.

"At twenty past nine last night Bill was having a drink with me after evening filming. That was in a pub called the Red Deer in the—"

"I know where the Red Deer is. Well, if that's confirmed—and you must both be pretty well-known figures around Leeds—that puts you both in the clear. Barring the possibility of time devices to set off the fire, of course. Tell me more about this evening filming. Who was involved?"

Liza thought.

"Bill and I. The Kerridges. Stephen there—the new curate—"

"Me," said Winnie. "Lady Wharton. And Marjorie, she's—"

"I know Marjorie. Anyone else?"

"Susan," said Philip Marston. "Our not-so-ingenuous ingenue."

"And Reggie of course," said Marjorie. "The Bradleys—just a few lines. Lots of extras, naturally. That's usual in the pub scenes. There was a time when the only black face you'd see in the *Terrace* was one of the extras in the pub scenes."

"The times they are a-changin'," said Charlie. "Slowly. So what time did filming finish?"

"Oh, about nine, I'd guess," said Philip Marston. But Liza Croome shook her head.

"No. Bill and I were in the Red Deer by a quarter past nine as I said. He and I were among the last to leave. Most people had just shot off, naturally enough. No one likes evening filming. I'd say Reggie called a stop to it about eight forty-five or fifty."

"I see," said Charlie slowly. Timing could be of the essence, he thought, and he distrusted their obviously fallible memories. "And were you and Bill Garrett the only ones who went to the Red Deer?"

"Oh yes. It was a heart-to-heart."

"So in theory anyone else could have been at Bridge Street where the fire was by, say, nine twenty?"

"In theory," said Carol Chisholm. "But many of us have wives, husbands, partners, parents. We could all have people who could vouch for our being home by then."

"Of course," said Charlie, with a suppressed sigh that said he really didn't need to be taught to suck eggs. "Now, one last thing and I'll take myself off. Bet Garrett implied that several of you here had slept with her. 'Touched her' was the expression she used—rather a nice, genteel way of putting it, that. If any of you want the fact to remain private, if possible, hold your peace and tell me when I or one of our people interview you later today or tomorrow. But if you've no objection to its being known, or if it's already well known . . ."

He paused and looked around. Harry Hornby, or rather Les Crosby, who played him, raised a finger.

"Me. Not a nice experience. Never repeated."

"Right. Thank you . . . Oh, Mr.—"

"Marston. Philip Marston. Peter Kerridge in the soap. It's well known to all the cast, I should think. It lasted—what?—half a week. Three or four days. Not a grand passion."

Charlie looked around and saw that Marjorie had made a tentative signal to him.

"Not me. But Vernon Watts and she were on-and-off—so to speak—lovers. She was available whenever he wanted her, if she hadn't anything better on the horizon."

Charlie looked around the group for a last time, registered that there had been no lesbian confessions, then let out a deep breath.

"No more, then? Thank you very much. The list may need enlarging, so I'll keep it open."

Chief Superintendent Collins sat in his chair staring ahead of him with distaste and feeling very superintendentish. On the other side of the desk Chief Inspector Birnley was trying not to squirm, but Collins was sure he was squirming mentally, and he was glad.

"Let's get this straight: you went to the press conference intending to announce that the two dead people were Hamish Fawley and Bet Garrett. Why?"

"Why? Well, I felt sure they were the two, and thought that the press had a right to know."

"Any copper knows that we tell the press what we think they'll find out anyway, not what they imagine they have a right to know."

"I thought having the names in the public domain could bring people forward who had valuable information."

"You thought having two *Jubilee Terrace* actors instead of just the one would make it twice as big a story. What did you think when you saw DC Rani at the door of the pressroom trying to shove a piece of paper in your hand? That he was advertising a bargain sale at British Home Stores?"

"Oh, it was just that uppity twerp Rani trying to make himself important. I was concentrating on the press conference."

"I bet you were. But you somehow didn't think that, as Rani was intercepting you at the door of the press conference room, it was likely that his note had something in it that you should see before you spoke to the ladies and gentlemen of the press?"

"Oh, I thought it was just that full-of-himself Paki making a lot of a little."

"He's Indian. And he wasn't, was he?" Birnley was silent. "Was he?"

"I suppose not."

"He—on orders from Peace—was trying to stop you making an almighty fool of yourself. And you went ahead and made one."

"I'll put out a statement—"

"You'll put out nothing. I should by rights remove you

from the case. You can stay in nominal charge, orchestrate the course of the investigation, in close collaboration with Peace, but you will *never*, repeat *never*, give another press conference on this case." Or on any case, Chief Superintendent Collins said to himself. He looked long and hard at Birnley. "Is that understood?"

There was a long, hostile silence. Then Birnley shifted in his chair.

"Understood."

Filming was starting (a schedule was not to be put aside, not for a little thing like a pair of bodies) and the informal meeting between Charlie and the cast of *Jubilee Terrace* had broken up. As he was wavering over which corridor would take him to the office of Melvin Settle, the script editor, he was caught up by Garry Kopps.

"Going anywhere nice?"

"I thought I'd have a word with Mr. Settle."

"Nice-ish."

"But you're top of my list of the cast members I want to talk to."

"I won't ask why. It'll be my reputation as the *Terrace*'s intellectual. Or maybe the fact that I'm the only male in the cast who hasn't been with Bet Garrett."

"Really? And why would that be?"

"I'm sure you know the other part of my reputation, Inspector. My tastes lie in another direction. Mind you, I think that even if I was hetero I wouldn't be in the least attracted by a granite-breasted and granite-voiced tart like Bet Garrett."

"I don't think I would either."

"Wife and kidlets at home, Inspector?"

"Wife, Felicity. Children: Carola nearly five and Thomas six months."

"It sounds a real idyll. Pity: there are so many gay policemen these days, and soldiers too, that it's a real bonus if uniforms turn you on. But it doesn't sound as if I could possibly persuade you to 'absent thee from Felicity awhile.'"

Charlie sighed.

"If only you knew how often I've heard that joke."

"I'm sorry to bore you. You must live in cultured circles."

"I do. Felicity used to do teaching for Leeds University English Department. Every one of her colleagues tried the joke at one time or another, and every one of them thought they were being original."

"Sounds like the acting profession. We all spill over with quotations, usually from plays we've been in. Well, I'll give up any thought of seducing you. It's so long since I had a boyfriend it's like an automatic response to try it on with anyone young and attractive. Fancy a coffee?"

He gestured toward a dispensing machine. Charlie flinched.

"Couldn't we run to a canteen cup from a percolator?"

"The canteen will be full of cast who aren't filming, discussing the second coming of Bet Garrett. The coffee is vile from that machine, but there's a nice little alcove round the corner with a view over the Burleigh Road and complete privacy. It takes your mind off the coffee."

Charlie nodded, and in a couple of minutes he was sipping a cup of coffee that was every bit as nasty as the ones in the Millgarth Police Headquarters, and looking out on a view that was also not much better than the one there.

"You wanted to talk to me, I'd guess," he said. Garry Kopps smiled, not at all ashamed or embarrassed.

"Yes, I did. I guessed that underneath that cool and rather intimidating exterior there was a mind that was meeting with a crowd of actors for pretty much the first time and panicking at the newness of it all."

Charlie didn't readily admit to panic, so he just smiled neutrally.

"And soap actors are a thing apart, or many of them are. If you went and talked to actors from any theater company they could almost all make a fair fist at roles over a pretty wide spectrum—some would be roles they were made to play, some would be roles they could fit themselves quite comfortably into."

"So they could play King Lear and Sir Andrew Aguecheek and anything in the latest sitcom on telly?"

"Exactly. You sound as if you have had some stage experience."

"*Twelfth Night* at school. I played Sir Toby, though I shared the role with a well-stuffed pillowcase. It was billed as the first all-black *Twelfth Night,* as if that excused it. The bookings were so bad we canceled the public performances and just played to the school. They booed and threw things."

"Why all black?"

"Because we were. Top to toe. Brixton."

"Oh, I see."

"Get on with the soap actors. Why are they so different?"

"Because some of them aren't exactly actors at all.

They've played the working men's clubs, they've done acts for children's parties, they've even made good after being extras onstage or on television. One way or another they've got the acting bug, but they aren't really actors, and many of them can only play a tiny range of parts not very different from their actual selves."

"Any examples?"

"Well, Vernon Watts was the best example from *Terrace*. He was a third-rate comedian in the music halls and clubs. When he got the job he used to play Bert Porter as a third-rate comic. Used to complain if any of his scenes didn't have a joke in them. The scriptwriters usually complied, because it was easy. The joke could be as bad as they liked, because the point about Bert Porter was that he thought he was hilarious and wasn't."

"I get you. Who else could you say has this limited range?"

"Well, Winnie Hey, and probably Les Crosby, who plays Harry Hornby."

"But someone like Hamish Fawley was much more of a real actor?"

"Oh yes. To take an obvious point, he was playing a homosexual but he didn't have a gay bone in his body, and he did it very well, in private sincere and straightforward, in public a bravura caricature of stereotypes, especially when he was playing with homophobic characters. He could play competently a wide range of parts, but probably no one role would show any great depth or empathy."

"I think I get you. Who else would come under this heading: Bill Garrett?"

"Oh yes. Like the rest of us he wonders whether he couldn't have made it big in the real world of the theater."

"But why don't they—you—branch out?"

"Children, for one thing. And Bill until recently had an expensive wife. But as often as not the real reason is timidity. They look at that comfortable bank balance and they ask themselves: 'What would I do without it?' It's like being on the *Titanic* and instinctively keeping close to the lifeboats. Some of us made a big brave decision when we decided to be actors. Now we *are* actors, our native working- or lower-middle-class caution has come into play, and it tells us to stay in our cushy beds, safe and warm, and warns us that if we were professionally stretched, we might not stretch well."

Charlie thought.

"That means, I suppose, a lot of nervy, frustrated, neurotic actors, aghast at the lack of challenge in their work—pretty much like the rest of us."

"Pretty much, yes."

"Does it also mean that the most stable and contented ones are those who, by and large, are acting characters similar to themselves?"

Garry shook his head.

"Not really. They quite soon get the notion that they are actors, and get the notion too that they should be given bigger and bigger challenges. It's like Fortinbras thinking he can play Hamlet."

"So the result is very much the same?"

"I suppose so."

"Or is this just you generalizing out from yourself,"

said Charlie in his friendliest voice, "and making every-one else out to be as mixed-up as you are?"

Garry Kopps shrugged.

"You pays your money and you takes your choice."

"Well, I would not class Marjorie as a neurotic," said Charlie. "Nor Winnie, come to that. Verdicts on the rest will have to wait till I get to know them better."

And he got up and, directed by Garry, went in the direction of the chief script editor.

CHAPTER 9

Scripting a Death

＊

"Sit you down," said Melvin Settle, gesturing Charlie toward an upright chair with arms on the other side of his desk. The office was papered with photographs, and also had a sort of map that seemed to be charting the present and future plotlines of *Jubilee Terrace*, major and minor. Charlie, with another wave was given permission to get up and examine it closely. When he sat down again he said, "I'm interested in why Hamish Fawley was asked back to play in *Jubilee Terrace*."

Melvin Settle frowned.

"This keeps coming up. What's your problem? It was natural enough. We'd sent Cyril off to San Francisco—or was it L.A.?—anyway, to somewhere appropriate. But it made sense to bring him back to die."

"Did it? You could have simply said he'd died over there. Lady Wharton could have flown over for the funeral. Or he could just have been forgotten. Hamish was the sort of cast member who no one in the series would want brought back, or so I'd have thought."

"Christ, yes, you're right about that. You saw him, didn't you? If I'd had one more sneer at my scripts because they weren't Ibsen or Strindberg or whatever he tried to convince us he was used to playing, I would have—well, kicked his arse."

"Most cast members seem to have felt like that. So who invited him back?"

"Oh, Reggie . . . Wait, I've got it." He paused, feeling there was need for an explanation. "There's so much writing, rewriting, replotting, taking out sick actors, or ones accused of drunk driving or indecent assault, that I get muddled. It's not all regular, prearranged progress from A to B—sometimes plotlines simply get forgotten, or get overtaken by events, including events in the outside world. That's what happened then."

"What? Something got overtaken by events?" asked Charlie. Settle nodded. "What event?"

"The death of Vernon Watts. Bert Porter. That was back in June or July."

"I thought Watts was a—sort of—background actor. Someone's who's around, and commenting on important story lines, rather than a character who's important himself."

"He was, but characters like that still have to be given a proper story line now and then," said Melvin. "Often it's something quite minor: a relative comes to stay and can't be got rid of. Some minor character is suddenly given the conviction that she's got cancer. But on occasion it can be something quite major."

Charlie thought.

"I'd guess Vernon Watts's plotline was minor," he said.

"Why do you say that?"

"I've just heard Mr. Kopps's assessment of Watts's talent as an actor."

"Well, that's probably quite accurate. You can trust Garry's judgments. Vernon couldn't have coped with a strong story line. This was just a side issue to much stronger stuff: Vernon, or rather Bert, had taken on paper deliveries for Harry Hornby. We like to keep abreast of social changes. These days newsagents find it difficult to recruit paper boys and girls. Pay isn't good enough for the greedy little buggers. So often pensioners are taking on the jobs."

"Yes, that's happened in Slepton, where I live," said Charlie.

"Right. Well, the story line was that Bert was getting interested in one of the paper girls—not sexually, we wouldn't touch anything like that. Leave that to the Australian soaps. She's just standing in for the daughter he and Gladys never had. And she plays along with this, because she's a kind kid—the kid in the plotline, not the actress. This is the sort of plot you can close down any time you like: Bert has a heart-to-heart with someone who tells him what a fool he's making of himself. End of story. End of part for young hopeful playing the girl."

"But the plotline never got filmed?"

"Exactly. Vernon fell under the bus."

"So what happened?"

Melvin shrugged.

"Nothing much. It wasn't urgent. The story was going to develop very slowly. It had just begun with a little solo conversation between Bert and the girl: 'What are you doing at school?' stuff. It ended, I remember, with Bert saying, 'I never did well at school, but it hasn't done me any harm later in life.' A bit pathetic, that, with Bert earning the odd quid delivering papers, and the girl knowing it . . . Come to think of it, that may have been the last time Bert spoke in *Jubilee Terrace*."

"So what happened when news of his death came?"

"Well, we all knew we—the scriptwriters, that is—had to put on our thinking caps for something to take its place."

"Who came up with the solution?"

"Reggie, actually. Not one of the scriptwriters. He just handed us the idea and told us to get writing."

"But why Hamish? Why bring back Cyril Wharton?"

"All he said was that Hamish was available. He often was."

"But you'd never taken him up on it before? Brought Hamish back for a fortnight's holiday, visiting his old mum?"

"No . . . You'd have to ask Reggie, but I think he'd seen that the cast needed a shake-up. They get slack and lack-luster doing the same thing over and over again, the same clichés, the same facial expressions, in the same settings. Another thing is that Reggie got very little cheek from Hamish. Far less than me, or the other actors. So he could investigate this shake-up for the rest without being disturbed by it himself."

"I see. But as far as plots were concerned it meant two disasters in a short time."

"We made very little of Bert's death, just because the

replacement stuff with Cyril might include a funeral as well. No scene by the grave, just Gladys and her mates in the Duke of York's, discussing the service."

"I see," said Charlie thoughtfully. "I'm beginning to get an idea about the scriptwriting team. It sounds as if you have to negotiate with the actors, or at any rate field demands from them for story lines that feature them, or that they think would give them good opportunities."

Melvin Settle roared with laughter, though he didn't entirely convince Charlie he was wrong.

"Then I'm afraid I've given you a very odd impression. Yes, they come along to us with bright plot ideas, always featuring themselves. No, we don't negotiate with them. We placate them and send them away with the idea that we'll think about it. The older ones, of course, know that that's the last they'll hear of it. Occasionally they come up with a good idea. In the nature of things that's bound to happen: they've lived with the character, often for years. In that event the actor will probably go on a daytime chat show boasting about his brilliant idea. But in general we've got ideas and to spare, ten scriptwriters, and the idea has to be *really* brilliant, and to fit easily into the *Jubilee Terrace* format and ethos, to be taken up."

"I see. And how would you describe the *Jubilee Terrace* ethos?"

"Ordinary people leading ordinary lives, which some-times—more often now than in the past, because of the Australian soaps—get caught up in extraordinary events."

Charlie considered this reply.

"Can you tell me some examples of people trying to

plump up their parts in the show—some story line or incident that they've been pushing because it would make them more pivotal in the show?"

"Oh well, we could take Bet Garrett—now, I'm told, risen from the dead. Black mark to you boys in blue there, eh? By the way, if she hadn't risen from the dead I'd have done a quick rewrite so that her part in the shop scene could have been taken by Sylvia Cardew, the apprentice florist in the shop. It's a bit pathetic, isn't it? I hear she's probably the woman who died with Hamish."

"Tell me about Bet Garrett."

"Oh, it was a couple of years ago. She's been in (or rather in and out) of the show for almost as long as she's been married to Bill. At one point she wanted to be shunted out of her florist's shop and given something less *occasional* to do."

"She mostly comes in for births, marriages, and Mother's Days, I gather."

"Exactly. And making-it-up-to-her days for the men, which have been fruitful stamping grounds for her. Anyway, she fancied herself as landlady of the Duke of York's, or one of the residents of the Terrace houses. No way was it going to happen."

"Why not?"

"Not versatile enough, and not punchy enough. Odd that, because in real life she's got punch and to spare, but all her acting career, such as it is, has been playing fairly genteel, sensible middle-class women. Playing all the qualities she's never had. Very odd, as I say. Maybe she's got more acting talent than I thought."

"Did she offer her favors as a return for this promotion?"

"A bit late for that. I'd had her years before—sometime between her second and her third child. I remember because when I heard she was pregnant with the latter I had to do some fevered mathematics. The girl's not mine. Anyway, Bet hadn't anything in that line left to offer, and apart from sex her cupboard was bare. Boy! She'd have to have offered a lot to be landlady of the Duke of York's, even if we had wanted to be rid of Bill and Liza, which we didn't. The landlady of any soap pub is the lynchpin."

"Of course she is," said Charlie. "Usually pub land-lords and landladies last about five or six months in the real world these days, but that wouldn't suit a soap, would it?"

"Not at all," said Melvin cheerfully. "We're selective about how far we catch up with the real world."

Charlie shifted in his chair.

"While we're on the subject of recruitment and promo-tion of actors in *Jubilee Terrace*, there is the question of the dead girl."

"Oh yes. Well, actually, I'm not the person to ask about casting. Occasionally they do ask me to look at two or three actors when there are auditions for a new charac-ter, and I go along and tell them what we scriptwriters have in mind, and which way the character will go. But mostly I stay out of that. Often I don't see the new peo-ple until I watch the finished version of their first scene. I have no idea how this girl was picked out for the apprentice florist. I only know that when Reggie asked me to write one in—give her a line or two as well as an appearance, he winked and added, 'Something nice for Hamish.' The florist-shop scene—people ordering wreaths for Cyril—was actually filmed before the final shot of Cyril's death was scheduled. As it is we're having to make do with the practice shots for the death, which were actually very good."

"Well, I'll have a talk with Mr. Friedman about that," said Charlie. He decided to become confiding. "I'm needing to get a lot of background before I even feel able to understand this new world. There's so much I don't know. I cling to the fact that two very unpopular cast members are now dead, and in one case there's no doubt it was murder."

"That's true," said Melvin slowly. "By the bye, I've never thought that Vernon Watts's death was murder."

"Why not?"

"He just wasn't important enough."

"To the *Jubilee Terrace* people perhaps. What about the great viewing public?"

"They rather liked Bert Porter, though maybe they were getting fed up with him. Too many terrible jokes. There was a fairly general degree of approval for Cyril Wharton. Too often homosexuals in soaps seem to take us back to the days of Kenneth Williams and Jules and Sandy. Hamish didn't do that, except where he was deliberately guying that sort of gay. You can't say he got into the part in any great depth, but at least he took the character seriously, and didn't invite sneers or sniggers."

"And of course you in the script department don't need to commit real-life murder," said Charlie, to lighten the end of the interview.

"Of course not. We can have a soap murder, or just a soap death. Or we can just have them move away. In Australian soaps they always seem to move to Perth or Brizzie, as they call Brisbane."

"I've always heard well of Perth, at least," said Charlie. "Perhaps it's a case of 'Tis a far far better place I go to now.' But I should go and look for Mr. Friedman—"

But he was interrupted by the door opening and the man himself, knocking belatedly, coming in. Charlie could have sworn that at the sight of him Reggie's face fell. Had he been aiming to get at Melvin Settle first, Charlie wondered, and persuade him to keep quiet about something? That would make sense. About what then?

"Ah, Melvin, I was wanting to talk something over, but it can wait. Good morning again, Inspector Peace. I'd heard you were back. Please feel free to come and ask me anything at any time—except when I'm directing in the studios."

There was an orotundity about the voice and phrasing that had not been there on Charlie's first visit, suggesting that the man could quite easily pull rank and get pompous. Or perhaps just that Reggie was nervous.

"That's very kind of you, sir. I'll take advantage of it at once if I may." Reggie tensed up a little, and it was a second before he nodded. "I wonder if you could tell me how Sylvia Cardew got her part as a florist's assistant on *Jubilee Terrace*."

"Yes . . . yes, I can. It wasn't the usual way, but it was quite . . . let's say it was quite an acceptable way. One that had happened before. I gave her the job on the recommendation of Hamish Fawley."

"I see," said Charlie. "Did you audition her?"

"Good Lord, no. The part was hardly more than an

extra's part. I never even saw her, then or since. I won't now, will I? Poor girl."

"I think, sir, you'd better tell me how it came about."

"Oh sure. But it can't be important."

"The girl is dead, sir. Murdered."

"Oh yes, yes, of course." His face fell. It was obvious Reggie felt rebuked and did not like the feeling. "Well, Hamish came to me a week or so ago and asked me if I could get a tiny part for someone. Said she had her Equity card. Hamish was, of course, finishing up his second spell of time with us, and in the nature of things was never likely to come back. I thought it was worthwhile keeping him sweet—keeping things in general sweet, that meant, because Hamish was the only source of sour among the present cast, apart perhaps from the young lovers. Anyway, I said I could think something up, maybe make her one of Rita Somerville's (that's Bet Garrett's) assistants in the florist's. And Hamish said that would be fine, and even thanked me."

"Was that rare?"

"Almost unprecedented."

"So what happened next?"

"I told the script team, then I wrote a little note to the Finance Department saying that whatsername—Sylvia Cardew—was to be put on the payroll for one week, this week, for the part of florist's assistant. I signed it and gave it to Hamish."

"I see . . ." said Charlie, his voice charged with significance. "I'm grateful to you for telling it so fully. But if you could have kept quiet about it you would, wouldn't you?"

Reggie dropped his eyes, then seemed to decide on a course of action.

"Well, wouldn't you, Inspector? There was something a bit sleazy about the whole transaction. Hamish, after all, never did anyone a good turn."

"You mean he'd got her a part, and would be demanding what I believe is called a quid pro quo?"

"I think you know perfectly well what a quid pro quo is, Inspector, and yes: that is exactly what Hamish would demand. I don't think I'm being oversensitive on this one, but I felt it almost put me in the position of a pimp."

"Then why did you do it, sir?"

"I told you, I wanted to keep Hamish sweet . . . I also recognized the name, thought she'd probably been an extra or had a small part of some kind with us before—you know the kind of thing: customer in the Duke of York's, a patient at the medical center. So I thought she'd have had *some* experience, knew our ways . . . What I mean is, I suppose, that I thought Hamish hadn't just picked her up on a street corner and promised her a part in *Terrace*. It may sound silly, but that *is* the sort of thing he could have done, in a spirit of pure mischief. But I felt pretty sure that wasn't the case this time . . . Poor cow: I wish now I'd turned her down flat."

Charlie was about to thank him when Melvin Settle spoke.

"You know, now I've heard the name I'm beginning to think I've also heard it before. Reggie, wasn't she the sweet girl who delivered papers, the one Bert Porter was to get a pure sort of crush on?"

"Search me. I didn't direct the scene they did together, though I saw the rushes."

Charlie felt mystified.

"But that was a schoolgirl, wasn't it?"

"Oh yes. But as I recollect it, the part wasn't played by a schoolgirl."

"Going by the skirt I saw in the bedroom Sylvia Cardew certainly wasn't an innocent schoolgirl."

"I think I'd better explain," said Reggie. "There is a certain sort of young woman who, with a little help from the makeup department, and costumes, can be made to look like an early or preadolescent girl. That's how Sarah-Louise in *Coronation Street*, when she became pregnant at twelve, could be played by an eighteen-year-old actress."

"Good heavens," said Charlie.

"Exactly. With boys, of course, that's much more unlikely because of the voice breaking. That's why in Benjamin Britten's operas the boys are always played by boys, but the girls are often played by a young adult woman who can be made to seem girl-like."

"Quite apart from other reasons," said Charlie.

"All right, all right. Anyway, I assume this Sylvia Cardew was of the same type as Sarah-Louise, and could quite simply be made to look twelve or thirteen."

"Which might have given added piquancy to Hamish's designs on her."

"Possibly. Though you mentioned a skirt in the bedroom that—"

"True. But it was just the sort that a preadolescent might wear when pretending to be a fully grown whore."

"Well, that's how Sylvia Cardew could first be hired for

an adolescent and then as a much older girl. And unless someone scanned the cast lists no one would have noticed."

Charlie thought for a moment, not getting up as he assumed was expected of him.

"I'm still thinking of the little-girl aspect, the special thrill that could have been part of Hamish's designs on her, if he was that way inclined."

"I've never seen any signs of that," said Reggie.

"Nor I," said Melvin. "Quite the reverse. His engagement to Bet Garrett suggested he was really attracted to very experienced sexual operators."

"The engagement was a red herring," said Charlie. "I gather there was hardly a soul who thought it was a genuine result of mutual attraction. In a sense the piquancy of a preteen is a red herring too."

"What do you mean?" asked Reggie. "You're the one who floated the idea."

"I mean it's irrelevant whether he felt a special sexual excitement at the thought of bedding young girls. He was the victim, after all. The important thing is whether anybody else might have guessed that he lusted after young girls."

The two men looked at him.

"You're thinking of Bill Garrett," said Melvin.

"I'm not thinking of anyone in particular," said Charlie. But in fact he was thinking of Bill, of his three daughters and of his protective instincts toward them. The fact that Bill could have thought his victims would include not only a possible predator but also his wife made him doubly interesting to Charlie.

CHAPTER 10

Private Lives

✳

"Dying like *that*!" said Maggie Cardew. "The pain! The terror!"

"It doesn't bear thinking about," said her husband. But he looked as if he could think of nothing else.

"She were a lovely little girl," his wife went on, dabbing at her eyes and looking as if she were in another world. "The sweetest and kindest thing imaginable when she were four."

"Aye. And what was she when she were twelve?" said Danny Cardew bitterly. His words provoked a storm of tears, and he regretted them. "I'm sorry, love. I shouldn't have said that. There's nowt to be done about all that now."

"But what shall we tell the policeman when he comes? We can't tell him we haven't seen her in the last eighteen months. She living in the same town an' all."

Her husband considered until the tears had died down. Then he said, "Them's difficult years. Our Fiona were a handful when she were that age. Most girls are.

But Fiona came through—look at her today. And worse girls come through, often. Something, we don't know what, meant that Sylvia just went off the rails."

"What are you trying to say, Danny?"

"I'm trying to say there's no earthly good to be had from hiding things from the inspector. He'll find out what she's been these last years. He might as well find out from us. If it helps him to catch the coward as done this, we'll have done Sylvia the last service we could do her. God knows, we tried."

His wife thought.

"Do you mean that Sylvia was known to the police?"

"Must have been, I'd say. Probably got a record. If it had been in t'paper no one would have told us. If she were clever about it and kept out of that sort of trouble, there's still plenty of men who could tell the police what she were and what she did."

"But do we tell him everything, then? It's like a sort of betrayal."

"It's no betrayal when Sylvia never hid owt. We tell him all we know. It's little enough, God knows. But at the very least we'll save the man's time."

So when Charlie knocked on their door prompt on two, after walking around the neighborhood and savoring the atmosphere of nicely aging semidetacheds with neat gardens of roses and peonies and the odd dated lavatera, he was welcomed, invited to sit down, and was showered from the beginning with information.

It was a sad enough tale. Sylvia had been a late addition to the family but one who, once arrived, was loved and probably spoiled by her three older siblings and by her parents. She was, they assured Charlie, the loveliest and most biddable of children until she reached about twelve, and then she went off the rails in ways that twelve-year-olds never knew about in the Cardews' younger days, leaving them at a loss at how to impose a discipline and set of standards that had been missing till then.

"It was alcohol, drugs, and sex—sex at twelve!" said Maggie. "And the more we tried to tie her down, rein her in, the more she deceived us, wriggled out, flaunted curfews—just really, like we said, went off the rails. She were so lovely, everyone said so. And then she were so impossible—wanting all the most dangerous things going, and screaming blue murder if she were thwarted."

"Which wasn't very often," said Danny Cardew grimly. "We knew how to say no, but we'd no idea how to enforce it."

"That must have been horrible for you," said Charlie.

"It were. In the end she moved out, or just disappeared, rather."

"When was this? How old was she?"

"She were fifteen. That's four year sin'."

"It was terrible," said Maggie. "Like the end of the world, our world. She couldn't even be discreet about it—not her. You'd go into the bathroom and the evidence would be left everywhere. I'd gather it up, though I hated doing it, touching it, and I'd dump it in her bedroom. But it would be straight back in everyone's view, like she was trying to rub our noses in what she was doing."

"And you have three other children?"

"Yes. Fiona, the eldest, moved out as soon as Sylvia

started going wild. Fiona said she'd been through all that herself, but she could see that Sylvia was going to be something else again."

"Didn't you try to get one of Sylvia's siblings to talk to her?"

"Oh, we did. You can take it, Mr. Peace, that we tried everything. Fiona it were who had a talk with her. She were that shocked when she came out she just said, 'I'd get rid of her, Mum. It's the only thing you can do and stay sane.'"

"Is that what you did?"

"In the end when we told her we were at the end of our tether she just vanished, like I said."

"Did you keep up any sort of connection with her?"

"She rang now and then. She called maybe once a year, always with something to boast about, usually things most decent folk would die to have hidden. After a time she didn't think us worth her while, and visits and calls stopped."

Charlie thought.

"You're saying she was a prostitute, aren't you?"

"Aye, we are," said Danny.

"Prostitutes don't usually have much to boast about."

"Oh, she could boast about her 'earnings.' No holding back there. It was another example of pushing our noses in it. And she'd talk about her 'varied clientele' with 'special tastes.' We hated her visits, tell the truth. We were glad when they stopped, God help us."

"Mr. Peace," said Maggie tentatively. "Could I ask you a question?"

"Of course. I'll answer if I can."

"Was the man she died with—the man whose flat she was in—connected with television?"

"Yes, he was."

"That's what the policeman who rang told me. Was he connected to one of the soaps?"

"Yes. He had a part in *Jubilee Terrace*."

The two looked at each other.

"Why I'm asking is that she was on about the *Terrace* last time she came to see us—well, not 'on about,' but she did mention it."

"Did she now?"

"Said she had a date fixed up with someone who was 'on the *Terrace* team.' I didn't know what she meant by that, an actor or someone behind the scenes, but I didn't care to ask and get sneered at. She was very uppity by then: called herself an 'escort,' which seemed to mean meeting men in upmarket hotels, with their special needs all marked out in advance."

"I suppose she mentioned no names or their parts in the soap?"

"Oh no, nothing like that. And it wouldn't have meant much to us. We weren't viewers of it, and we always avoided it after that. We really didn't want to see her if she ever got a part in it, knowing how she would have got it."

Her husband was frowning.

"Didn't you say Mr. Judson said something about the *Terrace* a few months ago, Maggie?" he asked her.

"Said he'd seen someone who looked just like our Sylvia on it, only it couldn't have been her because she was much too young. He said this girl had a scene with Vernon Watts. Danny and I remember Mr. Watts when he did the working men's clubs. And he used to be at the City Varieties, didn't he, Danny?"

"Aye. Never that good, though. More of a warm-up artist than a star. Died not long ago."

"I know," said Charlie. "I'd perhaps better tell you that your daughter did get a part—two, in fact—in *Jubilee Terrace*. So it wasn't all fantasy. It was your daughter doing that scene with Vernon Watts."

The pair looked at each other, bewilderment and pain in their eyes, not pride or satisfaction.

Liza Croome was making up in her bathroom. She was "opening" a new supermarket in Keighley that evening, and the punters who would be there would expect her to look as like as possible to her Sally Worseley persona. The supermarket had in fact been open a couple of months, and Liza had been assured that a lot of the regular customers would be coming. She put on the makeup with a practiced hand. She had "opened" a great many supermarkets. She had begun to see them as the churches of the modern era, the present-day equivalents of all those little nonconformist chapels that were run up cheap in the nineteenth century.

Liza lived alone at the moment. In fact, Liza had lived alone for long periods, and she thought she would soon come to prefer it. Her last partner, Denzil, a curator at the city's art gallery, had upped and left her on an impulse—easy to do because he lived lightly and had moved out, as he had moved in, with only two suitcases of possessions. He had said then, "You're a lovely girl, Liza" (he scorned political correctness), "but I can't find my way around Sally Worseley. And these days you're more often Sally Worseley than you are Liza Croome. Find out who you are and I might still be interested."

Liza had said "good riddance" and denied she might still be interested if he ever deigned to return. But at heart she agreed with him that she was an unmendable split personality. It was not for her a criticism or a joke. She rather enjoyed having two personalities.

She looked at her face. The light makeup she preferred covered the damage of the years less well than the heavier coating preferred by the studio's makeup team.

"I've grown old as Sally Worseley," she said to herself. "Or middle-aged. We've grown middle-aged together, Sally and I."

She looked at herself so often in a mirror that she knew every line on her face, could almost put a date on when they had come.

"I could make a map," she said sometimes. "Like one of those atlases with all the altitude levels."

She saw a new line—another little claw on the crow's foot. She leaned over and pulled the light cord. Then she stayed looking at the dim reflection of herself from the low light in the hall.

If I'm more often Sally Worseley than I am Liza Croome, she said to herself, what does that say about me and Bill Garrett? I always tell people he's my best friend but I don't in the least fancy him, and that's true—I think. And yet . . . and yet I *care* about him more, infinitely more, than I cared about Denzil, or about Ian, Francis, Neill, Mark, and all the others. They said hard things about me when we broke up, and it was all water off a duck's back. But if Bill had said them I'd have been really hurt. I'd have gone over them in my mind for weeks.

That suggests something, doesn't it? If I *care* like that it surely must be something like love. I may not want Bill sexually, but the caring shows how enormously important he is to me. I would never want to be Mrs. Garrett, but if he married someone else when he was free I'd be shattered. And the more important the new wife was to him the more shattered I'd be.

This must be more than friendship. And it means that I can't mention to the police the visit he made to the Red Deer's loo—the visit so much longer than usual—covered by a muttered "touch of tummy trouble" when he returned.

Carol Chisholm had got home half an hour before, and had already peeled potatoes, shelled peas (imported from God knows where) and got out the Sainsbury's chicken breasts in white wine and mushrooms—something both her husband and her children liked. The husband in question was meanwhile regaling her as usual with details of his day—more of them, if the truth be known, than she needed or wanted, though she was used to switching down to half attention.

"I said to him, I said, 'If you think that's a power screwdriver go to the cash desk and buy it, but I tell you, you'll never get a screw in with an electric plane.' My God! Some people!"

"I expect I'd just let them get on with it, even if they bought the wrong thing," said Carol in her comfortable voice.

"More trouble in the long run," said Malcolm. He always said this when she said that. And he usually followed it up with "How was your day?" as he did now.

"Rather eventful really," she said evenly. "Bill Garrett's wife was reported dead in a fire that was started deliberately. You should have seen the faces when she marched into the studio, large as life and twice as brassy. It turned out the dead woman was a young girl who'd had a couple of small parts with us. She was sleeping with Hamish Fawley, but if this was divine retribution for that, most people feel it was a bit excessive."

Malcolm had only taken in a little of this. He heard but didn't listen, especially to Carol.

"Sounds quite a day. Oh, I forgot to tell you this chap who said he wanted an electric screwdriver eventually walked away with a set of garden furniture—said he'd heard we are due for a hot summer next year."

Carol in her turn switched to full off. It was the only way. Every one in the *Terrace* knew she had married a bore, and she knew she had married a bore, and did not, at least with the surface of her mind, regret it. Her private life did not intrude on her life as a mildly well-known soap actress. Unlike poor Bill, whose whole time on the *Terrace* had been marked by Bet's exploits, her neglect of the girls, her attempts to secure a proper and long-lasting role in the soap. His marriage had been a sadly visible part in the tapestry of his private and public personae, and even his decision to divorce Bet would not wipe out that background.

As they were eating their meal, with her argumentative daughter at table with them and her son watching *Hol-*

lyoaks on Channel Four, Carol's husband suddenly said, "You know, now I come to think of it, someone said they'd seen something about the *Terrace* on the Northern TV news at one thirty. He was in his lunch break. Some kind of police press conference."

"That's right. As far as we can gather someone at Northern TV told the police that Bet was Hamish's fiancée and partner, and the police thickly assumed that the person who was incinerated with Hamish was Bet. Red faces all round when it was found out that the corpse was someone else."

"Wow! That's quite a story. I'll be telling it all tomorrow, because everyone will be interested."

"Well, get it right. I'll go over the details again at breakfast."

One of Malcolm's most irritating habits was getting things wrong that he had been told by his wife because of his habit of only half listening. He was always, with the other half of his brain, thinking of what from his not-very-fascinating life as manager of a B and Q store he would regale to his family next. Really, he was a very boring husband, and it could not be said that her on-screen life with her *Jubilee* husband was much more exciting.

Philip Marston himself was a lot more interesting, and had to suppress lots of areas of his personality to stick within the narrow confines of the character he was playing. Odd, thought Carol, that she had never even considered an affair with him. If one had happened she doubted whether she would have classed the affair as adultery. She would, after all, be sleeping with her *other* husband.

But she had never considered any such thing, perhaps because when she was with Philip Marston he was almost always playing Peter Kerridge, and was thus only displaying his boring sides. If I want "dull as ditchwater," she thought, I can get that at home.

On the evening of the day that he learned that his wife was dead and then that she was not dead, Bill Garrett's main concern was for his children. All three had been at school when the first news came through. He had been at home, having no filming that day. He had considered going to fetch the girls home, and then had thought better of it. His wife, after all, had over the last few weeks become no more than an occasional visitor to the family home. He could go and fetch them in the lunch break, by which time the story would not have broken. He could have some sandwiches and Coke ready at home, and then tell them all at once. By eleven o'clock he was profoundly glad he had made that decision. He was phoned from Millgarth station with the news that the identification was much less certain than had been first thought. He decided he could collect the children and bring them home at twelve thirty, the lunch break. That way he could prevent them from hearing the totally erroneous report put out by the police earlier. He would try to play down the fire as nothing to do with them. The children would get enough snide and sensationalized commentary from other children in the days ahead. They could then just shrug and say the mention of their mother was a colossal police boob. He tried to get from the policeman on the phone how he should explain the boob: Had there been an attempt on Bet's life that she had survived? The police-man at the other end, who sounded Asian, remained stum. His "we can't comment at this stage" sounded as final as a cement wall.

So when he had got his daughters around the table—a rare occurrence—he made sure they'd all got sand-wiches or the creamy cakes they loved before he started talking.

"I got you home because something has happened, and you're all going to have a difficult time at school, because other children will be talking about it, and will be asking for explanations, and that's going to be awk-ward and embarrassing."

"Why? What's happened? Is it Mum?"

"No. Nothing's happened to your mother. But for a time the police thought she was the person involved, and a very silly policeman announced it to the press, and it will probably be in the early editions of the *York-shire Evening Post*. They thought your mum had died in a fire."

"But why should they think that?" asked Angela. "If it wasn't her?"

"They thought it because it was at the home of the man your mother was—said she was—engaged to."

They took some time to digest this.

"Is that Hamish?" asked Angela.

"Yes. Hamish Fawley."

"Yuck," said Debbie. "He's the pits."

"How do you know?" asked Bill, trying to keep any urgency out of his voice. "Have you ever met him? Seen him?"

"No. Betty Chisholm's in my class at school. Her mother plays Mrs. Kerridge in *Jubilee Terrace*. I hear more about *Jubilee Terrace* from her than I do from you."

"Good to know your school time is so well spent," said Bill.

"But is Mummy dead?" asked Rosie, still wide-eyed from the announcement.

"No. It wasn't Mummy."

"Was somebody else with Hamish?" asked Angela.

"Yes. There was a woman with him, but it wasn't your mother."

He waited while they took it in, each one chomping on sandwiches Bill himself had no appetite for.

"Can I go back to school this afternoon?" asked Debbie.

It suddenly struck him that his second daughter was going to be an actress. She wanted to go back to school because she knew she would be the center of attention. She would have even more to offer in the form of information than Betty Chisholm. It was the impulse to bask in the spotlight that drove so many people, talented and untalented, into the acting profession.

"If that's what you want, darling," he said.

That evening, when Angela and Debbie were in their rooms upstairs and behaving pretty much as they did every day of the week, his youngest daughter, Rosie, seemed to follow him around, watch him, as if he were the cornerstone of her life, which she tried to keep an eye on for fear he would disappear. When finally, all chores done, he sat down on the sofa, Rosie climbed up and sat on his lap, something she had not done for months.

"Daddy, I'm glad Mummy hasn't died."

"Are you, dear?" Bill asked, then hastily amended it to: "Of course we all are."

Rosie seemed to want to be asked why she would have been sorry if her mother had died, and when she wasn't she told him anyway.

"Mummy's funny. She says funny things and does funny things when you're not expecting it."

"Yes, that's true enough."

"I know Angela has done all the Mummy things for Debbie and me, and we love her, but when Mummy comes, or when she was around when you were sort of married, she often said wonderful things that made me laugh out loud."

"Yes, she could do that sometimes."

"Daddy, are you glad she's still alive?"

There was only the tiniest of pauses, but Bill thought his daughter noticed it.

"Yes, darling. I'm very glad."

Shirley Merritt, who played Maureen Bradley in the corner shop in *Jubilee Terrace*, was not one of the show's players who fraternized. She went in when called in, did her scene or scenes impeccably, sometimes improving her dialogue, then went home, usually to paint. Her relationship with Garry Kopps, her screen husband, was excellent, and so were the terms on which she lived with the rest of the cast, with the exceptions of Hamish Fawley, whom she loathed as everyone did, and Young Foulmouth, whom she avoided with a fastidious pursing of the lips. She came from a family that regarded obscenity or blasphemy as one degree worse than passing wind in public.

Thus she avoided hearing of the murder in Bridge Street until late on the following day, when she rang up the head caretaker at the Northern Television studios about a briefcase she'd left behind the day before.

"It's somewhere here, Mrs. Merritt," he said. "Can't lay my hand on it just now, but I'll have it for you tomorrow. We're all at sixes and sevens here, as you can imagine."

So when she said she couldn't imagine, knowing nothing about it, she was given the news of the double murder, of the policeman who had assumed the female victim was Bet Garrett, only to find after the announcement of this fact that it was somebody else entirely. When Shirley heard who the victim was, she was mystified.

"I don't think I know her."

"She was playing an assistant to Mrs. Garrett in the flower shop," said the caretaker, for the twentieth time that day. "And just before Mr. Watts died he'd had a little scene with her as one of the kids who deliver newspapers."

"I don't think I know her. I don't watch," said Shirley. She added, but only to herself, that she thought Bet Garrett a much more likely victim than a girl still playing adolescents.

Shirley lived over a shop in Briggate in the center of Leeds. It suited her, as an observer of busy humanity who preferred not to participate. She went over to the window, where her watercolor pad was sitting on a table. It showed a half-finished picture of Briggate on a Saturday, with bustling, spending humanity on a late spring afternoon. It had something of the feel of Lowry, without his matchstick quality.

For her more experimental pictures she preferred oils. These pictures were by subject more in the manner of fifty years ago: abstracts or seeming abstracts that with prolonged viewing made real sense. She prepared a canvas, and got out her palette, which was always in a state of readiness. In the center of the canvas she started, in a violent, shiny red, to paint. The red assumed the shape of lips, half-opened lips. Soon she went on to off-white inside the aggressive rosebud shape, and they became two or three teeth, which somehow had an aggressive quality like a naturally quarrelsome dog's. Around the lips, in an order that was not nature's, there was fashioned first nostrils, unnaturally distended, then mascaraed eyes, blue and cold, then hair that made no pretense of being anything other than dyed blond.

At a small exhibition of her work in a gallery in Woodhouse Lane later that year, the occasional visitor from the Northern Television studios stood in front of the picture, and if he or she stood long enough they discerned a likeness to Bet Garrett: predatory, disaster-hungry, destructive.

Shirley the private, the withdrawn, the observing, had always seen Bet as a terrible source of evil and heartbreak. That was what came from the canvas: the quality of inhumanity that almost disqualified its possessor from being part of the human race.

The viewer who could see this wondered why Shirley Merritt seemed to have hated Bet so much. Because the force of the image led anyone who knew Shirley to question the depth of her supposed detachment from the world of emotions.

CHAPTER 11

Kinds of Loving

✳

"She was ace," said Sharon, sprawled on the large bed in her pad over a shop near the market. It was the second day after the fire. Charlie made notes from the depths of a Lloyd Loom chair that had been made oddly comfortable with the aid of two cushions. "She had everything, did Sylvia. She knew what she wanted and she knew how to get it."

"And was being a prostitute what she wanted?" asked Charlie, feeling he hadn't phrased that in the best way possible.

"Escort," corrected Sharon. "No, 'course it wasn't. Some of the girls enjoy it, but they know it's only short-term. A means but not an end, if you get me."

Charlie thought he should go more carefully.

"I think I get you," he said. "I suppose being an escort brings you a sort of independence and sufficient money—you hope—so you can start planning on being something else."

"Well, something like that," said Sharon. "But don't be obsessed with money. We're not. That's only part of it. I'd say it wasn't even the most important thing. I'd say the most important is contacts."

"Right," said Charlie. "But before we get on to them, could you give me some idea what sort of . . . escort Sylvia was?"

"Bloody brilliant," said Sharon. "She was up in every possible preference, if you follow me, and she was willing to do whatever it was that was asked of her."

Sharon, Charlie was finding, was a wonderfully communicative witness. He had half expected that. Sharon had heard the presumed identity of the other fire victim on Radio Aire in the eight o'clock news that morning. She had rung the police and told them Sylvia was her "best mate" and said she was willing to do anything to help them catch her murderer. People who do that are either true friends or anxious to deliver the dirt on a rival under cover of helping the authorities. So far Sharon had been undeniably in the first category. Indeed, she seemed to have taken Sylvia as her role model.

"So Sylvia was versatile, could minister to every taste," said Charlie.

"Pretty nearly," said Sharon. "Homosexuals didn't have much use for her, natch."

"I suppose not. She presumably earned a fair bit of money."

"A fair bit about covers it. She wasn't on the game for every hour God sends—she had lots of other interests, not like some."

"One of the interests would be acting, I suppose."

"Yeah," said Sharon, "that was the main one, no question." But she wriggled as she said it.

"Was she trained?"

"Nah. She started at that Manchester School or College, of whatever, but it got in the way."

"Of her . . . escort work?"

"Yeah. They didn't combine well."

Charlie felt he was being given the picture of a girl who was into high-class prostitution to put by a nest egg of money that would enable her to train as an actress, but she gave up the training to concentrate on her escort work. That hardly made sense, and he didn't get the impression that Sylvia was a muddled thinker.

"I suppose she was going to break into acting some other way," he said.

"'Course she was. Didn't you see her on *Jubilee Terrace*?"

"Watching soaps doesn't sit easily with a policeman's job. Either we're on duty and preparing for a busy night, or we're catching up on family life."

"Well, you missed a treat. She was brill."

"Her parents have just seen her schoolgirl scene. They found it very disturbing."

"I bet."

"It was like having the old Sylvia back, but they knew that at that age she was . . . quite different."

"I'll say. I met her back then, when she was in school. She discovered sex, or sex discovered her, when she started high school. Wham bang!"

She laughed appreciatively.

"This scene she had with Vernon Watts—"

"Is that the old git the wrinklies go on about? Used to be on the music halls—gasp, gasp. Cue for gypsy violins and sobs into grubby handkerchiefs. I don't get the sentiment. If it died the death, it must have been because it couldn't attract audiences. Where were the grubby handkerchiefs then? I'd bet the music halls were the last refuge of really *crap* comedians and singers, wouldn't you?"

"Probably," agreed Charlie. "By the end anyway. Did Sylvia talk about Vernon Watts?"

"She said he propositioned her."

"She must have had plenty of experience of that."

"Oh, she did. But she never let on about her escort work to Watts. It would have been round the cast, and done her no good, and especially not with the powers that be. She just turned him down flat—she'd got experience of that too, though you might not believe it."

"I do. Sorting out clients into the safe and the dangerous is one of the escort's first priorities. But what did you mean, 'done her no good'?"

"I mean in getting on in television. That's what she wanted. She'd had a client a couple of years ago who'd promised to get her on. At the time she'd gone on and on about that, how she couldn't wait, and so on. Then he'd been written out. It devastated Sylvia. And it was a real humiliation, because she'd gone on about it so much. She kept stum when the chance came again."

"Was this another of her clients?"

Sharon shook her head.

"Same one, so far as I know. He was pulling strings from abroad. So the chance came again. Sylvia was brilliant at doing children—for clients, I mean, those that were that way inclined. And she auditioned and got this part in *Terrace*. She was over the moon."

"She only had a short scene, didn't she?"

"That's all she'd done so far. She was promised that this relationship was going to develop over the months, and the old git was going to get obsessed with her. She knew all about *that,* did our Sylvia. She was devastated when he fell under a lorry or whatever it was."

"Was that the end of her TV career?" asked Charlie, thinking the role of innocent might pay dividends.

"I don't think so. She told me a week or two ago that she'd got another part lined up in *Terrace*."

"Same girl or different?"

"Different. They couldn't think of anything for a twelve-year-old so they gave her some other part more her own age. No more than a few words, though, in the script."

A new idea struck Charlie.

"Was she under contract?"

"Yer what?" It was a surprising descent into Sharon's native dialect.

"Did she have a contract with Northern Television for a certain period?"

"I dunno. But she mentioned six months a lot."

So she'd got much more than Reggie had let on about.

"Right. So maybe she got this second role, as a florist's assistant, to give her some employment in the time for which she already was under contract."

He'd strayed beyond Sharon's apparently formidable know-how.

"Search me. But I bet the git who'd got her the earlier job took all the credit for the later one."

"Why do you say that?"

"Because he was like that. A lot of the clients are. They take credit if you pick up a five-p piece off the pavement."

"Are you saying you knew him?"

"No. I'm saying Sylvia talked about him a lot."

"Did she give him a name?"

"No. We don't if we're talking about clients. It's a question of confidentiality, and not getting robbed of good customers. We invent names sometimes. Syl often called this one Mr. Fixit."

"I see . . . because he could get her jobs on TV?"

"Because he said he could."

"Seems to me he'd proved he could."

"S'pose so."

"Did she tell you anything else about him? About his sexual tastes, perhaps?"

"No. We like to keep quiet about that. Confidentiality again, but also to protect our territory. Say I make a specialty of some service that one of my best customers always requires. It doesn't do to be too open, too explicit-like. Someone else can go after this customer and persuade him she could give him an even better service."

"So you don't know anything more about this man who claimed to get her jobs?"

"Not that much." She frowned, trying as always to give satisfaction. "I think she liked him as a customer. He could do something *for her,* instead of it always being the other way round. I think often money didn't change hands, but promises did. And he was as good as his word, wasn't he? He got her the jobs. But I don't think she liked him as a person."

"Why not, do you think?"

"Too sarky. Always getting some sly dig in. Always reminding her of what she did, and how a lot of people wouldn't think it a legit trade. As if Syl would care about that! He enjoyed hurting people, even people he liked. Was he the man who killed Sylvia, do you think?"

"I think he may have been the one who died with her."

Sharon thought about this. She was a girl who would have puzzled Charlie if he had not come across many prostitutes in the course of his work. Her speech varied from coarse street jargon to quite sharp argumentation. The background that she came from and the class she now mingled with were fighting a messy battle in her mind. Charlie had no doubt about her attitude to Sylvia. There was no question she admired her, but he wondered whether she actually liked her: there were traces of jealousy in her tone, and Charlie had no reason to think that Sylvia had been a likeable person. He thought that probably ever since Sylvia had discovered her body at the age of twelve she had had the driving ambition of using it to get wherever she wanted to go. And it had got her to that charred bedroom in Hamish Fawley's rented accommodation.

"How would you sum up Sylvia?" he asked, getting up.

"Dead clever . . . sorry, I didn't mean that as a joke. She had an ambition and she kept her eye on it. And she would have made it, I know she would. She wouldn't let anything hold her back."

"And you? Will you take your A-levels? Will you get a job worth doing?"

"Yeah. I'll do it. In time. There's plenty of time."

"Well, don't be like Sylvia: she dropped out of education."

"I guess she thought she could get the same career perks for far less hassle."

Charlie sighed. That meant Sylvia had preferred to be on her back to sitting at a desk. He wouldn't mind betting that Sharon would make the same career choice.

"Where are you on your way to?" Felicity asked Charlie.

"Ilkley," said Charlie into his mobile. "I'm just approaching Ben Rhydding."

"Nice place, Ilkley."

"I've always liked it. But I won't be taking the waters."

"Harrogate cured you of spa water."

"Whenever I'm in a spa I thank the Lord for my hardy stomach."

"Who are you talking to?"

"The guy who supervises the scripts and writes a lot of them. A chap by the name of Melvin Settle."

"Ah. Wrote two goodish mainstream novels around about the mid-eighties. Couple of sci-fis since then, no great shakes."

"What it is to have a wife who's into literature. I'll bear it in mind. Could be a self-loathing intellectual who despises himself for slumming it."

"Are you any further?"

"An inch or two. It doesn't help that we have two possible intended victims. It doesn't make for clear thinking."

"I'm just sorry for the girl."

"Thought she was sleeping her way to a meaty part, and instead found herself burning her way to an early grave? It's not quite like that. A bit more complicated. The tabloids will all be on to it by tomorrow or the next day. Save your tears till you've got the whole story."

"What would we do without the tabloids? They save us an awful lot of tear shedding. How old was the girl?"

"Nineteen."

"I think I'll shed one or two."

When he got to Ilkley, Charlie, who believed in doing his work in advance if possible, drove confidently through the handsome and busy center of the small town and then up one of the roads leading to the moors. It never did a policeman any good arriving at a suspect's house poring over town guides or listening to sat.nav. and peering at numbers on gates. If seen and in plain clothes he was put down as a burglar immediately.

Melvin Settle was certainly not a suspect, or at least not in the front line of them. Everyone connected with *Jubilee Terrace* had a wisp of a cloud of suspicion hovering over them, but Melvin had struck Charlie as amiable, clear-headed, and inclined to be helpful. Up to a point, he corrected himself. Most of the people connected to *Jubilee Terrace* seemed with part of their minds to be protective of the soap, of its popular image as actor-friendly as well as viewer-friendly. It liked having the reputation of a place where a new actor is welcomed with smiles and hugs, and one who is getting past it is eased out with tact and follow-up care. Since after night duty he was often stranded at home with only daytime chat shows,

Charlie was used to seeing new characters and much-loved veterans telling the nation what a lovely and talented lot they all were, and how working on the team was an unmitigated joy.

Funny about the murder then.

He stopped confidently outside Moorland Hill, number 24. It was a commodious nineteenth-century house, designed for a Victorian family with several servants—stone, solid, exuding comfort and durability. Melvin did pretty well out of his commanding place in the *Terrace* hierarchy, then. Probably not regretting his well-thought-of mainstream novels at all. Charlie could hear nothing from the road, but as he approached through the well-kept front garden he heard the sound of a child screaming—what he, with his own children, called "creating." This sounded like a much older child, though—probably a teenager. As he rang the doorbell his stomach rumbled, and he wished he'd stopped for a sandwich.

"Yes?" shouted a woman's voice as he rang the bell.

"Inspector Peace, Leeds CID. I'd like to speak to Melvin Settle."

"You're welcome . . . MEL!" she screamed up the stairs, then when steps were heard on them, seemed to go up to comfort the yelling child. Charlie was kept waiting a minute or so before the front door opened.

"Ah, Inspector Peace. I wasn't expecting you. Do come in. We're having a bit of a domestic at the moment, nothing we can't cope with." He led the way through a high, dark hall, then when they were halfway up the stairs screamed at his wife, up in the attic area, "Keep that bloody child quiet. She should be at school."

"Oh yes?" came the female voice. "Infecting the whole school, I suppose?"

Melvin shut the door of another high room, this time a handsome one with oak bookshelves covering whole walls, and plenty of easy chairs.

"Becky hasn't got anything to infect them with," he muttered to Charlie with a conspiratorial wink. "One day Irene will realize this happens every second Tuesday, when she has to either hand in or get back physics homework. I bet she hasn't done any for the last six months. Either nobody has noticed or nobody has bothered."

Charlie wondered why Melvin had not enlightened his wife about this, but he decided not to ask. He had no ambitions as a marriage counselor and he had enough questions that were really relevant. He sat down in one of the capacious armchairs, and Settle sat at his desk, fiddling with a pen.

"What can I do for you?"

"I'm interested at the moment in Mr. Friedman."

Settle shrugged.

"Oh yes? Then why don't you go and talk to Reggie. He's been very open with you so far, hasn't he?"

"Apparently so. But I think one of my ancestors must have been a crab. I like to approach things sideways, get a nice mass of information so that I can judge a person's answers. Probably you do the same with new characters on the *Terrace*. Now it strikes me, thinking back on several conversations I had at Northern TV's studio, that Mr. Friedman was one of the people who was really closely involved with Hamish Fawley."

"Does it? I don't think he'd quite agree with that."

"But he gave me all the necessary information about their relationship: he had brought him back into the soap, he had been willing to employ someone (admittedly in a small part) entirely on Hamish's say-so. If he gave Sylvia Cardew the role of florist's assistant after Hamish had brought his influence to bear, then quite probably he had given her the role of the newspaper girl for the same reason—the influence, then, being exercised from London, Hamish being out of the series at the time."

"I wouldn't know."

"Not necessarily, no: casting isn't your job. And then there is the question of two years ago. I've been talking to Sylvia's best friend—also in the same profession. She says that Sylvia had real hopes of a job in *Terrace* two years ago—confident of a role, sure it was in the bag. Then the chap who was getting it for her was written out and nothing materialized. What does that suggest to you?"

Melvin shifted uneasily in his chair.

"That Hamish was doing the pushing then too."

"It does seem likely, doesn't it?" said Charlie genially. "What else does it suggest?"

"Look, I'm not Reggie's best mate or anything like it. It's not up to me to say what it suggests."

"Fair enough. Well, *I'd* say that, to the outside eye, it suggests that there was a close connection between the two—not necessarily friendship. It does seem as if Hamish Fawley was quite incapable of friendship—didn't *do* it, so to speak. But there surely must have been *some*-thing, and the likelihood is that it was either some matter that Hamish held over Mr. Friedman, used as a weapon to get what he wanted. Or else that there was a community of interest between them, something that was criminal, or bordering on it, that both of them shared."

"Something like this came out in our last conversation, Inspector."

"It did."

"That was while Reggie was with us, and it really concerned Hamish and his tastes."

"That's right. But people with way-out tastes tend to . . . cling together (I can't think of another expression)."

"But the fact is," said Melvin, "that neither Sylvia Cardew nor Bet Garrett were children, and only Sylvia could, let's say, childify herself through makeup and clothing."

"That's right . . . You once told me, sir, about the ethos of *Jubilee Terrace*. Ordinary people in ordinary situations which sometimes become extraordinary."

"That's roughly it."

"How does that translate into the show's PR, or the studio's PR about the show?"

"Well . . . that's not my business, but . . . it's cozy, our PR. It plays down the fact that the show is made by actors and plays up the parts they play. We want to make it a family thing—family viewing, with characters of all ages so that several generations can find things of interest to them in it."

"That's what I'd have said from watching interviews with cast members on daytime chat television."

"Oh God! Daytime television. Why do you bother?"

Charlie refused to be sidetracked.

"I would have thought that the sort of actor that goes

down well with the PR department is Marjorie Harcourt-Smith, and maybe (I haven't met him yet) Bill Garrett—chunky, dependable, right-minded: the sort of person everyone would like as their next-door neighbor. Or of course their pub landlord."

"Yes, I think that's true. Where is this leading?"

"Whereas they would be much less interested in someone like Garry Kopps, who's not only a pretty good actor but he's also gay, and writing a book about soaps which isn't fan fodder but a serious analysis of their appeal and what we seem to be calling their ethos."

"Yes, I can't recall Garry ever having been on *This Morning* or the *Richard and Judy Show*."

"What I'm getting at is the cozy, 'invite us into your home' aspects of soaps, or this soap, with actors and characters merging into each other, and a feeling of everyone being at heart rather nice."

"You make it sound pure escapism, but I suppose it's true."

"So the PR department would be pretty upset not only if a character or even a behind-the-scenes man was arrested on charges that were definitely criminal (pederasty, let's say), but also if it was something that was perfectly legal sexually but had an aura about it of the ridiculous or the unsavory."

"Yes, I suppose they wouldn't be happy."

"So you don't know anything about any of the cast or the background boys that could have been used in that way?"

"No, I know of nothing. If I did I would have told you."

"Would you, sir?" said Charlie, raising his eyebrows.

"Well, not while Reggie was in the room, but in private."

"I ask because there hasn't been much probing in that direction. But Sylvia Cardew's previous part—the adolescent paper girl—should have alerted us."

"Yes, yes. I see that now."

"We have two possible intended victims here: one of them was a full-time prostitute with an interest in acting—or at least in getting a high-profile television part. She was just into her third projected role in *Jubilee Terrace*, one of which never quite happened. These could have been brought about by a bit of genteel blackmail by Hamish Fawley. Or more likely by a concerted piece of genteel blackmail by the two of them, Hamish and Sylvia, of one or more members of the *Terrace* team."

"I hope you're not suggesting—"

"I'm not suggesting anything. I'm looking at possibilities. And I'm trying to work out why a tawdry soul like Sylvia Cardew, whose only gift was an ability to play children as well as girls of her own age, could wield such influence on the second-most popular television soap."

Melvin said nothing, looking into the middle distance. Then he shook himself.

"I wish you well in trying to find out the truth. You'll be trawling in some pretty murky waters."

"Most of the waters I trawl in are murky." Charlie stood up and went to the door. "Are you a devoted family man, sir?"

Settle looked up as if he were going to break out into an apoplectic response. Then he swallowed and spoke softly.

"Five. We have five children. I was very slow to realize that that was far too many. I have no particular affection for children, Inspector Peace. I was with them all evening on the night of the murder—or, rather, they were with me. Shouting, laughing, fighting, galumphing around the house, they and their friends, possibly making love, with me fuming every five minutes without even creating a temporary five minutes' truce. Oh yes, I could not have burned that sad pair to death—not me, a devoted family man. Or, as I prefer to call it, familied man."

But Charlie's thoughts, as he drove back to Leeds, had strayed from the subject of sex with children. He had talked all the time of two candidates for the role of main intended victim. He must never ignore the likelihood that in fact there were three.

CHAPTER 12

Wife and Mother

✳

The room where Bet Garrett had settled bore every resemblance to a cheap hotel room, if such still exist. The building called itself a guesthouse, but it was no more friendly or welcoming than more grandly designated buildings. There was a tiny box with a wash basin and shower, and the main room contained so much useless furniture that you grazed your calves and shins whenever you moved around. The three-quarters bed seemed to be permanent home to an open suitcase, from which items could be taken as they were needed, and from which dirty washing spilled on to the eiderdown.

"Sit down," said Bet. "You make the room seem small."

"It is small," said Charlie. He was in no mood for sexually tinged compliments about his size.

Bet was not, at that moment, an enticing figure. She had apparently just emerged from the shower, in which she had washed her hair, and she wore only a blue bathrobe, loosely tied to draw eyes to her full front. Charlie's were duly drawn, but the breasts didn't materially alter the general impression of a sloven trying to be voluptuous.

"I've got to get down to finding a permanent place," she said. "I'm just here because a friend took pity."

The friend presumably owned the Otley Road Guesthouse, not far from the cricket ground. It bore all the hallmarks of going through a bad patch, and Bet's person and slatternly habits seemed to encapsulate this.

"You're not thinking of going back to the family home, then?" Charlie asked.

"Am I heck as like! I suppose I might if Bill handed it over lock, stock, and barrel, and with vacant possession."

"You're not interested in custody of your daughters?"

She grimaced.

"Enthusiasm for that is pretty near rock bottom. I suppose at a pinch I might take them on, if Bill paid a hefty sum for their upkeep. Kids' clothes cost the earth, and these ones eat like horses as well, usually from takeaways. It's not that I need the money. The custody claim was just a laugh at Bill's expense. He thinks the sun shines out of those girls' backsides. I'd screw money out of him for pure pleasure, to pay him back for I-don't-know-how-many years of marital boredom."

"I see," said Charlie, neutrally, he thought. He was not neutral on the subject of daughters, since he loved his elder child to bits, in spite of her tyranny over him.

"Oh, don't get me wrong about my brood," said Bet, trying a hefty fluttering of the eyelids. "They think I'm a hoot, and they love me in their way. Their dad always gets things badly wrong. He used to read them fairy stories which bored them rigid because what they really wanted was *The Simpsons* on video. He'll be doing the same sort of things now he's on his own with them—taking them to the *Lord of the Rings* when what they really want is *Pirates of the Caribbean*. Poor old Bill. Always the loser."

"You don't seem to have been on a winning streak yourself recently," said Charlie. Bet's eyes widened dramatically, to make her look like a Disney stepmother.

"Eh? What's that mean?"

"I mean splitting up from your fiancé, then losing him in a fire."

Bet sighed.

"Bloody sight better than losing myself in a fire," she said. "What do you see before you? Nine stone four pounds of pure womanhood raring to go. If me and Hamish had stayed together there would have been me in that bedroom, and you'd have been looking at charred remains. I'm grateful, thinking it over, to Hamish and that Sylvia Whatsit."

"Do you think you could have been the one the arsonist aimed at?"

The reply was definite.

"No. Anyway, it doesn't do to think like that."

"Why do you say no?"

She looked at him pityingly.

"You stupid or something? How long have you been on this case? Don't you know that Hamish was the most hated man on the set? He made it his business to put people's backs up. I'm the same—that's what drew us together for a bit. We like to make things happen, and deliciously unpleasant things too, as a rule. But compared to Hamish, I'm Mother Teresa."

"I'm pleased to hear it. How *did* you two come together?"

"Well, he knew who I was, of course, as I knew him. He'd been in for about a year, then he was written out. He'd seen me with Bill, as well as all sorts of other men. He probably had a good idea what sort I am—game for anything, that's my motto. When he came back in he came in on a scene we were filming outside St. Peter's Church in Northwick. He was delighted when everyone showed quite clearly that he was the last person they wanted written back into the series. It was quite funny how unanimous they were—except for me. I just watched and thought: There's fun to come from this."

"And he saw you were different, and you got talking."

"He just came over and asked me out for a drink."

"And did the idea of the engagement spring from that?"

"A bit later, actually. Good ideas take time to mature." She let out a cackle of laughter. "But we took to each other at once—and we slept with each other from the start too."

"Was that unusual?"

"Pretty much standard practice, actually."

"What sort of person was Hamish from the sexual point of view?"

"Try everything and do it regular. He wasn't highly sexed so much as variously sexed."

Charlie thought about this.

"I think I understand. What about children?"

"What do you mean, 'what about children'? He didn't *want* any."

Charlie sighed.

"Was he interested in sexual acts with children?"

She screwed up her face. "Sure to have been. Just his line, screwing up the helpless and the vulnerable. Targeting their weaknesses, making them laughingstocks. He'd have slept with lambs and calves as soon as eat 'em. But live lambs and calves are rare in Leeds."

"So was there any relationship between Hamish and your own children?"

She looked at him, twisting her face with distaste, possibly genuine, possibly assumed.

"No, there was not. I made sure not to have them round while I was living in Bridge Street. It may surprise you, but I don't act as pimp for my own children."

"So you draw the line somewhere?"

"*Yes.*"

"But you might have used Hamish as one of the key elements in gaining custody. 'M'Lud, the plaintiff is shortly to marry, and will be able to provide a stable environment in a two-parent family, so important for growing girls'—that kind of garbage."

She thought for a time, her mouth working as if she were chewing gum.

"I thought along those lines for a time. But as I've told you, that was just a game at Bill's expense, whether he realized it or not. I was never going to go the whole hog—not to court or wherever. I had had him squirming, and that gave me a big laugh. I was always going to withdraw the action and leave those three little angels as a rich gift to Bill."

"You sound scornful of him for wanting them," said Charlie, still the father of a daughter.

"I am." She thought, and then said, "It's not as though he can be sure all of them are his."

"Oh. Are *you* sure?"

"I could make informed guesses."

"Maybe it wouldn't make much difference either way. Maybe he just loves *them*."

"You're probably right. That would be just like Bill. What a wanker!"

Charlie decided to pocket his own little obsession with fathers and go off on a slightly different tack.

"How did you meet?"

"Bill and me? In a pub in the center of Leeds. Can't remember which one. Quite posh."

"How long ago was that?"

"How old is Angela?"

"I don't know. I haven't talked to her."

"Well, around fourteen. No, wait—it's October. Say fifteen. Add nine months and you've got it. We actually married when I was seven months gone."

"Were you in love?"

"Of course I wasn't. I've never been in love. Not daft enough for that."

"So why? To get a job in television?"

"Yes, maybe. Bill had been in *Terrace* for a couple of months then. That's how I recognized him in the pub as an actor, and that's why I started to talk to him. I'd taken a few acting classes at the College of Music and Drama. I had dreams, ambitions . . . A fat lot of good Bill was to my brilliant career."

"You got a part in the series."

She shrugged, sneering.

"If you call that a part. I'm called in now and then, when they need flowers for an occasion, and someone with a genteel Yorkshire accent to complete the scene."

"I don't recognize your accent as genteel Yorkshire."

A vocal change came over her.

"Do you not? Well, it would probably surprise you to know that I went to two excellent schools, St. Ethelburga's, near Knaresborough, and the Thornton School for Girls, near Bradford. No expense spared. My family at the time was on an upward curve."

"What went wrong?"

"I think I recognized, if they didn't, where I naturally belonged. And that was on the streets. I had been expelled from both those excellent schools before the penny finally dropped with them. By then I spoke the accent of the streets for preference, and I've remained a streets person." She went back to her preferred brogue. "Common as muck, that's me."

"It sounds as if you were rather young to get the part of a shop manageress," said Charlie.

"Oh, I didn't start as the manageress. Bill introduced me to the casting people. I started as a shopgirl—genteel Yorkshire shopgirl in a very nice trade, daughter of the manageress, who took over when her mother retired. I suppose that slut Sylvia Cardew was hoping to rise by a similar route."

"Is that the slut you're so grateful to?"

Bet stuck out her tongue like a naughty schoolgirl.

"Yes. It takes one slut to know another . . . *Sylvia*, though! Would you believe it? *No* one is called Sylvia these days."

"I think it was her actual name."

"There you are. Why couldn't she change it to Sharon or Kerry like all the other girls who want to get on in the profession?"

"Getting back to your marriage," said Charlie, who thought he was being led onto the paths of madness, "you stayed married to Bill for fifteen years, but with a few interruptions when you had other men, is that right?"

She smiled in unashamed self-adulation.

"I had them queuing. Don't ask for a list. With most of the men at Northern Television I've simply forgotten whether we did or we didn't."

"In the meantime you had these children, paternity uncertain, and you had occasional acting jobs, while your husband was permanently under contract to the makers of *Jubilee Terrace*."

"That's right."

"Why now?" asked Charlie urgently, trying to break down the wall of self-love. Bet thought for a few seconds.

"I take it that you mean why did the marriage finish just at this time? Well, you can take so much boredom and squabbling back and forth. And you can take only so much of being expected to look after three brats, and feed them and wipe their dirty mouths—not to mention their dirty backsides. I got tired of domesticity, that was it. It had nothing to do with Hamish's reappearance. The engagement and custody stuff was simply a wicked ploy to drive Bill out of his mind. I wanted to launch myself out on my own. And I never, repeat *never*, will get married again."

Charlie nodded and thought hard.

"Were you often called in to play this part as florist?"

"Maybe once every three months or so."

"Was it usually one day's work?"

"Sometimes. They'd usually pay for more, to cover retakes."

"And this week? You were called in for how many days?"

"Two days, but they paid for four."

"And I gather you filmed with Sylvia Cardew."

"Right."

"What was your impression of her?"

"Go-getter. I should know. I'm a go-getter myself. And there's no way a go-getter is going to offer a helping hand to another go-getter."

"And did she seem to think you might?"

"Not really. She had a much more effective ally than I could ever be."

"And who was that?" asked Charlie, knowing.

"Who do you think? Hamish, of course. I was absolutely flabbergasted. When a new face appears we all try to be nice to them. Company policy. So I asked about what she'd done, and of course she didn't mention having been—still being, I gather from gossip in the canteen— a high-class whore. But she did say she'd had another part in *Terrace*, and that just a few weeks back. One of Harry Hornby's newspaper deliverers, with a story line in the offing when Vernon—Bert Porter, this is—takes a shine to her. That was torpedoed by Vernon being careless in the London traffic. Then she told me she'd had a part lined up eighteen months ago, one involving Cyril Wharton. Hamish. So she'd had three parts allocated to her, all different, two of them substantial ones, at least prospectively. 'Who's a lucky girl then?' I said. She could see I was boiling. I wanted to say, 'How long did you have to lie on your back to get those?' but luckily held back."

"You must have seen lots of new cast members in your time. Why were you so annoyed about this one?"

"Why do you think? Because it was all due to bloody Hamish. I'd sweated blood to try and get this bloody jerk to give me a part worth playing, a real flesh-and-blood woman, preferably mostly flesh, and all the time he says maybe and makes a little gesture with his hand like he was waving me aside and saying forget it. And this little slut has him just where she wants him, over a period of months or years, and she gets landed with these nice roles, and the powers-that-be wink at all the difficulties involved in having her as an eager schoolgirl one week and an enthusiastic young apprentice the next. Oh, it makes me mad, I can tell you."

But you're not holding back on it now, thought Charlie.

"Aren't you missing something out?" he asked.

"I don't think so."

"Hamish didn't allot roles in *Jubilee Terrace*."

"No, of course he didn't. I don't *know* how he went about getting his whore roles, but the proof is in the results. She did get them."

"Then he must have used somebody."

"Oh, he did that, all right."

"Who would you put your money on?"

She thought for a moment.

"It's got to be Reggie, hasn't it? There's Melvin too, I suppose: he is sometimes called in about casting. But really, that's not his responsibility. He's wholly intent on getting a good script together: one full of one-liners, piquant situations, interesting confrontations. He knows Northern Television has a great storehouse of potential performers and they won't let him down by getting a no-hoper for any role, however small. I'd go for Reggie."

"Right. Here we have the most unpopular man in the cast, loathed by all—much more than the young people are loathed, or Vernon Watts was. And yet someone, maybe Mr. Friedman, caves in and agrees when Hamish comes up with a suggestion for a new role."

"She said her ten words perfectly adequately in our scene together," said Bet, unusually gracious, which interested Charlie. "She must have done all right in the role of the preteen-ager. That's a special gift. Maybe Reggie respected Hamish's judgment where actors and roles are concerned."

"And pigs may fly and cats hate cream," said Charlie. "You've changed your tune, but it won't wash. Hamish had a weapon he could use. Call it blackmail, call it vigor-ous negotiation, he knew something, had power over some-body, that he could use: maybe it was Friedman, or Settle, or maybe someone I haven't been introduced to yet."

Bet shrugged.

"Maybe. I wouldn't know."

Charlie exploded. He knew when he was being played with.

"You wouldn't know? You were engaged to the man, you were living with him periodically, you were pressing him to get you a better part in *Terrace* and yet you had no idea *who* he had to influence to get it for you, or what he would use on that person to get his way. Do *you* think that makes sense?"

"Makes sense to me. That was how it was. Take it or leave it."

Charlie's eyes narrowed.

"I'll find out, don't you doubt that. Two more questions: How did your engagement to Hamish break up?"

"Just naturally. I told you what the engagement was for—to scare the shit out of Bill. We'd done that, we'd had all the fun we could have out of a pretty unlikely pairing that nobody but Bill really believed would come to anything. So we brought it to an end."

"Without any rancor or rows?"

"Absolutely amicably."

"And what were you doing on the night that Fawley and Cardew died?"

"I was here in the hotel. There's no bar here—it's what they call 'no frills,' but you can find frills if you have a nose for them—Freddie runs a sort of impromptu bar down in the basement. I was there all evening, till midnight or later. We had fun. He's a mate."

Charlie said nothing, of acceptance or nonacceptance, merely nodding and leaving her bedroom. He aimed first for the breakfast room, down in the basement. It was a large room, much larger than was needed for the number of bedrooms. It was dismal, as all such rooms are except at rise-and-shine times. There was room for a bar, especially an impromptu one, but no sign of it, not there or in the attached kitchen. Bet's friend Freddie was nowhere to be seen, nor did Charlie find him in the dingy office that served as reception when there was anybody to receive.

The heavily curtained TV room, which called itself a lounge, was also empty. The hotel was looking after itself, and seemed to have gone so long without a spring clean that Charlie felt he would be in need of a shower when he got back to police headquarters. He let himself out of the guesthouse and walked slowly to his car.

Most interviews of suspects left him with questions to be answered, and the talk with Bet had left him with more than usual. Her pride in herself as one who made things (mostly nasty things) happen led him to the thought that she was a much more likely target for a murderer than Sylvia Cardew. Maybe she was a joint target: her point about Hamish being by far the most hated member of the *Jubilee Terrace* team was fair enough—but they made a perfect pair: not either/or but both. And there was the important point that Bet had been around, acquiring and discarding lovers and enemies, for a long time: fifteen years. Hamish had had one period when he was high-profile in the series (one year) and now a brief return (about six weeks). Hamish was hated, but he had had less time to arouse detestation and fear. On the other side of the scales could be put the fact that Hamish did not waste time when he was bent on making enemies. But then there was the surely vital fact that he was about to leave the cast again, this time for good. Why kill him now? The thought struck Charlie in passing that it was strangely lucky that there had been a run-through of Hamish's death scene, and that it had been recorded.

There was another oddity about the interview. Why had Bet been so notably unforthcoming about how

Hamish had wangled jobs for his protégée, a girl with lit-tle training or experience, whose chief recommendation seemed to be the faculty of being able to look much younger than she was?

Come to that, Charlie thought: How had Hamish got a return engagement himself? There had been talk about shaking the company up after Vernon Watts's death. But surely the downside of Hamish's return heavily out-weighed the upside? Everyone hated him, he caused rows and unpleasantness, and that surely was not the sort of atmosphere that benefitted the cast of a family soap. Cyril could very easily have been left to die in California—if, indeed, he needed to die at all. Why did he come back? Why, to put the matter more precisely, was he brought back?

If he was using some knowledge, perhaps some skill he possessed, to pressure the powers that be, or one of them, most likely Reggie, to force them to employ him again, then his murder could have been undertaken to rid that person of Hamish's threat. Bet had denied being privy to whatever gave Hamish his power. Well, she would, wouldn't she? And if she had somehow discovered Hamish's powerful secret it was easy to guess that she was silent on the matter because she was aiming to use the knowledge to advance her career.

Very tempting, that. Very dangerous too.

CHAPTER 13

On Location

✳

Things were looking black for Colin Cooke. Colin was seven, and had not attended the marriage of his soap mother with Arthur Bradley (known to his friends as Garry Kopps)—officially because Maureen had been worried about how her former partner would take her marriage. For the same reason she had made no moves to alter her son's last name. Maureen had responded well to marrying into the corner-shop trade, being a cool but obliging presence, knowing where everything was, and responding to requests to "put it on the slate" with the absolute authority of "There is no slate." She was always nervous, however, when her ex-partner Brian Whiteley's name came up. As any faithful viewer would suspect, she had good reason to fear her ex. It's tough being a child in a soap, and particularly so in *Jubilee Terrace*. Few babies in the cast had got through their early years without being the victim of at least one kidnap attempt. Young Colin was lucky to have got as far as the age of seven, but there were reasons why a kidnap had not been scheduled earlier.

Usually the kidnap involved a high place, with anxious faces watching from the darkness below. The high place this time was St. Aidan's, a church the soap had never used before, due to the hostility of its vicar to any attempts to go down-market. That vicar had died, however, and the new one was eager for any publicity he and his church could get. So now, in the cold night of an October Friday, the tower was floodlit and up in the tower (how he had gained access was one of those inconvenient details usually skated over by soaps) was to be seen by glaring lights the figure of Brian Whiteley—Maureen's ex—looking suitably demented. He clutched in his arms a large child with his face concealed (the child was enjoying himself enormously) and occasionally shook his fist at heaven in a manner that many thought had gone out with the late Henry Irving.

Down below Shirley Merritt and Garry Kopps, as mother and stepfather, were emphasized by the positioning of the crowd. Their faces registered every shade of apprehension and concern. Mingling in the crowd around them were Bill Garrett, Carol Chisholm and Philip Marston, Susan Fyldes and James Selcott, and quite prominent was Stephen Barrymore, the Terrace's new man of the church. Also quite prominent, though he didn't want to be, was Charlie Peace.

He had picked up talk of the evening filming when he went back to the TV studios after his rather frustrating interview with Bet Garrett. He knew the filming would be policed, but he thought he could probably mingle and pick up what people were talking about between takes. On the way there he dropped in at police headquarters and collected PC Hargreaves, who was just going off duty and was dressed in civvies. He was delighted to get the job, which would provide talk in the pub after the next match of Leeds Rhinos. Charlie was used to not taking into account his own color, which was just how he liked it, but there were some circumstances where that was unwise. A white, middle-aged policeman in jeans and anorak was much more likely to be able to stand casually near *Jubilee Terrace* actors and listen in on the conversation than a young black one—who in any case was by now known to most of them.

They arrived during a lull. They saw Maureen Bradley's feared former partner put down the stalwart child, who was immediately pulled away from the parapet's edge by a safety expert. The partner, Brian ("Call me Bry") Whiteley, was played by a New Zealander, but he was exhausted by the run-through and he walked up and down the narrow space shaking his arms and clenching and unclenching his hands. He seemed to lack the inexhaustible energy of most young people from Down Under.

"Went well," Charlie heard Philip Marston saying to Garry Kopps.

"Not bad. This is my third hostage-taking but the first time Arthur has been closely involved. I've learned by watching the others. I suppose you've done the same. People in soaps know there's nothing new under the sun."

Charlie was about to send Hargreaves to mingle with the crowd when he realized that he needed to be told who in the mass of Leeds humanity were the actors, who the extras, and who the fans roped-in unpaid. He had just got to Marjorie as Gladys Porter when he stopped.

"What's the matter, guv?" Hargreaves asked.

"That's Bet Garrett who plays the flower shop manageress."

"Wife of Bill, who plays the pub landlord—and the one who was announced by that prat Birnley as being one of the victims."

"Good—you're getting it. She and her husband are separated, and she'd been sleeping with Hamish Fawley, who died."

"So? Why did you stop?"

"It's just that I wouldn't have expected Bet Garrett to be one of this crowd. She exists in the cast to sell flowers for weddings and funerals. She's not a fully fledged *Terrace* star by any means. Make her your first priority."

That was easier said than done. Bet was on her own, watching the goings-on with a half smile on her face. She seemed not to want to be talked to, and those around her seemed to be happy to leave her unapproached. One or two of them, in fact, looked at her askance, as if she were responsible indirectly for the two recent deaths. One person, whom Hargreaves had been told was Liza Croome, seemed to be staring at Bet with particular loathing. He dallied, waiting, thinking Bet might take out a mobile and give him something meaty, but she stood, relaxed, that little smile on her face, and before long Hargreaves felt he should move on.

He came to rest beside Peter Kerridge and Gladys Porter—Philip Marston and Marjorie Harcourt-Smith, he had been told. Bloody upmarket name for a *Jubilee*

Terrace actress, Hargreaves thought. Hargreaves's patchy experience of the *Terrace* told him that the Kerridges and the Porters were the *Terrace*'s oldest families, backbone of the series, though sometimes shoved aside for a bit when the action shifted to the new, less central characters. They embodied the fine traditions of the soap, or so publicity would have said.

Then Hargreaves said, Hold on, to himself. He had remembered something. He had read about another of the actors, Vernon Something-or-other, and thought there had been some question about his death. At the time he'd thought that he might have seen Vernon in person in the distant past, on one of those occasions when his parents took him to their working men's club in Bramley on a Saturday night.

"He'll want to go up the tower, to set up the next scene," said Philip Marston.

"Oh yes. He'll want to get it right," said Marjorie.

Hargreaves was alerted not by the words, but by the studied neutrality of the tones in which those words were uttered. Nothing that could be objected to, said in a manner that itself said nothing. He committed the words to memory, using techniques from a memory-improvement course he had taken years ago, before going on to the Advanced Computer and the How to Win Friends courses. Hargreaves always felt better for his courses, and was uneasy if for any reason he did not have one on his current agenda.

"It is the climax to the month's episodes," said Philip Marston. "And it's difficult, with the child. He has to get it just so."

"Oh yes, that's what I meant. He'll probably do several takes, and take the best of each one."

"Rather them than me," said Marston. "I'm glad to be just a face in the crowd."

Hargreaves tried to see if they had their eyes on anybody. It was quite obvious that they didn't. In the darkness of the churchyard their eyes went from person to person as the conversation continued. Then Hargreaves changed tack. He tried to note whom in the little crowd around the base of the church tower the two actors *didn't* look at. That would be the natural equivalent to the studied neutrality of their words and voices. He soon realized that the person they did not look at was just the one they would have been expected to be most aware of.

They never looked at Reggie Friedman.

Reggie was wearing heavy black glasses, a chunky brown pullover, and weathered jeans. He was going here and there in the knot of people closest to—but not very close to—the church itself. The fans and ordinary people who had been hauled in to make up the numbers were given the more obscure placings; the characters who had words to speak, important reactions to be filmed, were moved to within the scope of the street lighting. When he had everyone and everything to his liking he turned and strode theatrically toward the church.

"There he goes," said Marjorie, but in a voice that was scarcely more than a whisper. Hargreaves looked around. Charlie was wandering through the crowd, noticing everything but talking to nobody beyond a nod or a "good evening." He obviously was keeping his eye on his sergeant, and the next time their eyes met Hargreaves jerked his head in the direction of the deserted part of the churchyard.

"Quick," said Charlie when they met up. "I want to see what's going on up that tower."

"So you should," said Hargreaves, "but I doubt you'll be able to. The studio's heavies are keeping everyone this side of it."

"So I've noticed. I thought of saying, 'Police,' and flashing ID but that would make me more conspicuous than I want to be. Why did you say I should be watching the tower?"

"This Marston man and the Porter woman—"

"I've noticed you listening in to them."

"—they've been talking about Friedman, how he will be sure to go up the tower, and so on. They've been saying it in voices so totally drained of meaning or individuality that it seemed suspicious in itself. Do you get me?"

"I think so. Gossip and innuendo, but sounding like a speaking clock."

"Less informative than a speaking clock. I'll give you the details later. See you after the filming."

Charlie was surprised at Hargreaves's enthusiasm for this job. He had only ever known him to get excited about Leeds Rhinos and their Saturday results. Charlie looked around him. All the *Jubilee* cast members and the extras were looking fixedly at the east side of the church tower, the side nearest the street and the lych-gate, a disconcerting appendage to the church thought up by its Victorian architect R. Prentice Prenderghast. The parapets on the other three sides of the tower were almost entirely invisible, and tape and security guards kept the crowd to the one side of the churchyard. Charlie sighed. To go and ask permission of the security guards to enter into the forbidden area of the churchyard would make him the most looked-at man at ground level. He grimaced. Nothing to be done. Glancing around he saw that Hargreaves was listening in to James Selcott, who was on his mobile. Charlie was willing to bet he was speaking to Susan Fyldes, who was on her mobile in the other corner of the churchyard.

"Keeping an eye on your tame poodle?" came a voice in Charlie's ear. Standing beside him was Stephen Barrymore, the curate who had suddenly taken over as the representative of spiritual values in the soap. He looked inoffensive but lively as usual.

"If you want to think of it like that," said Charlie. "Hargreaves is more like a rottweiler than a poodle in my eyes."

"We don't like police in Australia," said Stephen. "Corrupt as hell, and vicious with it."

"People say it's getting like that in this country," said Charlie. "But I don't think we're any more corrupt than the Church of England."

"Don't take me as a symbol of the Church, for God's sake," said Stephen. "I've never even been christened."

"Are you just here tonight because the whole scene's taking place around a church?"

"No, I'm not. Much better and more lucrative than that. I have a vital role in the action."

"Fair enough, I suppose. We do quite often use ministers of religion in hostage-takings."

"I'm told," said Stephen, in his demure way, "that Leeds Metropolitan University has a course in hostage crisis situations management."

"Christ! That's a course in itself?"

"The use of men of the cloth features quite prominently in it, I'm told . . . Oh, there's Reggie. He's gone up the tower to do last-minute adjustments, I suppose. We should start filming soon, then he'll try to get it all over in a matter of twenty minutes or half an hour."

Charlie had fixed his eye on the tower, where Reggie was fussing with the New Zealand actor. He kept his eye on them, but kept the conversation on Stephen Barrymore. He noticed that the young man was already feeling at home in television work: he called Friedman Reggie, and knew all about the sequence of events in one of his filming sessions.

"You're nicely bedded down," he said.

"If you're hinting that I've been bedded down with Reggie I deny it absolutely. I'm not at all his preferred sex and I'm not at all his type."

"And what, may I ask, is his type?"

"I plead permission to be silent, being a minister and a representative of the All Highest on this earth."

"Bully for you . . . *Oh!*" said Charlie.

Reggie, talking to the supposed ex-partner of Maureen Bradley of the corner shop, had bent over and taken the child hostage into his arms. He now turned him around to give him a look at the panorama of Leeds after dark. Charlie saw for the first time that the boy was a Down syndrome sufferer.

"Yes," said Stephen, and he sounded almost parsonical.

"It's a bit surprising, isn't it? They pride themselves on being pioneers. He was the first Down syndrome child to get a part in a major soap."

"I'm fed up with firsts," said Charlie. "From what I hear *Jubilee Terrace* has token blacks in its cast, and the number of blacks never rises significantly above one." His eye strayed significantly to James Selcott. "I'm a lot more interested in percentages than in firsts."

"Ah, you're thinking of the hugely popular James," said Stephen. "Hugely popular with the public, that is. Pity nobody in the cast would put out a hand to save him from an oncoming bus."

"Ah, you're thinking of the traffic accident in *Terrace*," said Charlie. "Wait a minute, though. That wasn't in *Terrace*. It was in real life."

"Easy to confuse the two," said Stephen.

Elsewhere in the churchyard Bill Garrett, who had been avoiding his soon-to-be-ex wife, became aware that she was approaching him. There was no avoiding Bet when she was in a determined frame of mind.

"Hello, Bill."

"Hello, Bet."

"Why are you keeping out of my way? You've no reason to. You've heard from my solicitors, haven't you?"

"Yes, I have." He had been keeping out of her way so as not to feel the need to thank her. "Thanks, Bet. It's a weight off my mind."

"I bet it's weight off the little horrors' minds as well. Now they'll only have you to torment—and I bet they'll get their way one hundred percent of the time."

"Well, you won't have to worry your head about that," said Bill. "I hope to give them a happy childhood."

But he said it to Bet's departing back.

Sergeant Hargreaves had very good hearing. He had never ruined it by having crap music played at him at high volume in a confined space. So though while talking into his mobile James Selcott kept his voice low, Hargreaves, standing a few feet away, could hear every word.

"And what did my favorite piranha fish do with its evening?" James asked. "Did it go to some hideous club long since blackballed by all right-thinking young people of Leeds?"

"No, actually I didn't. I went to Club Monterey, with its crowds of fashionable youth."

"It's as I thought."

"And by the way, if I were you I'd try to avoid the word 'blackballed.' Rumor has it you are about as under-manned in that department as Adolf Hitler."

"Rumor, as usual, speaks false."

"And did my pit bull terrier friend find anyone willing to endure his perpetual monologue on himself and his prospects, or did he stay home and nurse his self-love in his usual isolation?"

"When I can find company suitably intellectual and talented I'm always happy to share myself with her. And did you have the company of your leading (and only) fan last night? And did you find his cretinous adulation perfectly to your taste?"

"He's actually with me now, and he heard that and—" She paused. "Oh, watch it. Shooting is starting."

Hargreaves, preparing to reconstruct the other half of the conversation from the half he had heard, noticed that too. Reggie Friedman was back on the ground and doing some last-minute rearrangements in the crowd, most of which seemed to give special prominence to Stephen Barrymore. So the Church was going to play a crucial role in the happy resolution. In soaps, hostage situations always involved the young and always were resolved happily. You really couldn't imagine a Down syndrome child being thrown from a church tower in a soap. There would be questions in Parliament and in general a gruesome mixing of fact and fiction the like of which had not been known since Tony Blair pleaded for Deirdre Barlow to be released from her horrendous woman's prison.

Cameras rolled, and Stephen Barrymore moved to his central position in front of the church's main entrance, carrying a loud-hailer. He raised it and began speaking.

"Brian, I'm here to help. We're all here to help. You've been to me these last few weeks, and I've tried to do all I can for you. The reason we want to help, all of us, is that we know you love your son. You do, don't you?"

There was an inarticulate choking sound.

"Yes, I know that because we've talked about it when you came round. Only last week. And you said you were off your head with worry because you were afraid Maureen wanted to stop you having access to Colin. Now I've talked to Maureen and she's said she would *never* do that. She's adamant about that, Brian."

There was a spate of invective from Brian Whiteley, in which the only comprehensible sound was "bitch."

"You know that's not true, Brian. You and she lived

lovingly together for six years. You've got to get it into your head that the only person threatening to take Colin away from you is yourself."

"I'd go too."

"What good would that do, if you killed your son? This is a terrible situation you've got yourself into—and got Colin into too. We come from the same part of the world, you and I. We love our children Down Under. We'd do anything for them, because we know they're our future . . ."

And so it went on. The scriptwriter had reproduced in condensed form the sort of conversation that goes on, sometime for hours at a time, at hostage-takings. Charlie, who had been at several, had no doubt that the nation would be glued to its screen. For once in a soap, a clergyman would be something more than a well-meaning twerp. A first! And Charlie had no doubt that the scene would be the making of Stephen Barrymore. The young actor in one leap would be transformed from drama student to nationally known face. Such fairy-tale metamorphoses were in the gift of Reggie Friedman and Melvin Settle.

Charlie strayed through the crowd, staying as far as possible from the cameras, but fascinated by the developing scene. Soon Brian was clutching his son again, and Charlie got another glimpse of the boy's plump, puffy face. He hoped if he and Felicity had such a child they would be able to love him or her as strongly as Brian Whiteley did—and more wisely, he added to himself.

Hargreaves, half a churchyard away, was finding it difficult to act up to his instructions. The crowd of extras and others was on its best behavior, and there were only brief exchanges to be heard between members of it, not extended conversations. He stopped trying, and slowly and circumspectly wheeled around to survey the scene. One member of the crowd had withdrawn from the majority and was now over by the lych-gate taking out his mobile. Hargreaves, who knew the churchyard well as a place where druggies congregated at night, made his way as quickly and silently as his bulk allowed around to a clump of trees a few feet away from the gate. It was a *Terrace* actor who he thought, from Charlie's introduction, was the pub landlord. Garrett, that was the name— biggish, potbellied, but with a lined and frown-marked face. He was the one whose wife that prat Birnley had announced as the dead victim of the fire, only to have her turn up at the TV studio. What a cock-up!

"Is she all right, darling? . . . You're sure it was nothing worse than a graze? . . . Yes, I know it's the kind of things kids like Rosie pick up in the school playground." Bill Garrett was totally absorbed, and now took a deep breath. "Yes, I'm an old worrier. You can be a pretty good worrier yourself, Angie . . . How are you then?"

The conversation got on to domestic details. The children had had something from the freezer for their "tea," and Angie had just put the two younger ones to bed. Rosie was still young enough to have a story read to her, and Angie had chosen one of her favorites. Hargreaves was nearly ready to pack it in, not being a domestic kind of chap himself, but he was pulled up by a note of steel in the voice in the next words.

"What's that?" he said, his voice still low, but strong.

"No, they haven't . . . I expect they will soon, but they seem to be concentrating on Reggie Friedman at the moment . . . No, I don't think he does, and nobody dares to tell him."

Garrett took another long breath.

"Angie, there's nothing for you to worry about. I had a hand-delivered letter from her solicitor saying she was withdrawing her claim to custody. If they come you can tell them what we talked about. You remember it, don't you? . . . You're a great lass, Angie. I don't know what I'd do without you . . . Looks as if the filming here is ending. Bar reshootings, I could be home in twenty minutes or so . . ."

The whole unreal scene was breaking up. Colin, the boy, was back down on terra firma and reunited with his real mother, to whom he was talking volubly. Others were drifting, or in the case of *Terrace* regulars hurrying, away to buses and cars. Hargreaves went toward his boss, confident he would have at least one nugget of information that would be of interest: it seemed that Bill Garrett had been coaching his daughter what to say to the police.

But it was later on the car trip back to the station, when his news about Bill Garrett had been received with grunts by Charlie, and also a "Well, you'd expect that: the innocent and the guilty prepare what they're going to say to us," that Hargreaves finally struck gold.

"You've met Friedman, haven't you, sir?"

"Oh yes. Before and after the murder."

"Would you say he was a likeable man?"

"Hmmm. Efficient, good at his job, every aspect at

his fingertips. But likeable—I never got any vibes that suggested he's that. Why?"

Hargreaves shifted in his seat.

"Looking at him up the tower reminded me of someone I once played rugby with. A big forward, no particular character that I knew of, and I can't say I disliked or liked him. Then, after I'd seen him with a mentally handicapped girl, daughter of one of the fans, I was told he was a man who got his kicks from sex with handicapped children. Kids of either sex, mentally or physically handicapped."

"What did you do?"

"I had no proof. I didn't do anything . . . This man, I couldn't go near him. I felt—revulsion I suppose is the best word."

"Difficult in rugby. It's a very *tactile* sport."

"I gave it up. I should have done that two or three years earlier, when I was really fit and still quite fast. But I've always remembered that chap . . . And seeing this producer chappie Friedman with the lad, holding him . . . it reminded me."

Charlie was glad that it had.

CHAPTER 14

A Special Case

Charlie enjoyed being on the road. He decided that he was a nature man at heart, though whether he would actually enjoy trudging through the fields and woodlands around him was another matter. He had just bypassed Keighley and was on the motorway toward Skipton, and the truth was he probably enjoyed driving fast through the nature he thought he worshiped. But some way up from Steighton he began looking for an exit road.

The rather primitive way led through a tiny village, then became a virtual cul-de-sac, with only dirty paths branching out in both directions. Charlie, who had talked to Keighley police, took the left path, bumpy but quite navigable, and eventually landed up in front of a stone farmhouse—perhaps eighteenth century, large but basic, and probably modernized inside into a perfect media person's residence, expressing every aspect of his personality and lifestyle as he wanted those two aspects to be perceived.

Just what he needed, Charlie thought, to get a handle on the enigma that was Reggie Friedman.

He left his car beside the other one—an old Honda Civic, small and dirty—in the dirt square that was the parking area. He sensed he was watched from a window, but he refrained from waving or smiling and rang the doorbell like a casual but not unfriendly visitor.

As the door opened slowly he could hear from a distant room a child crying. When it was fully opened he saw a small, thin woman in a baggy frock looking at him appealingly.

"Are you the police?"

Charlie flipped around his ID card, and she looked at it with interest.

"Detective Inspector Peace," said Charlie. "Is Mr. Friedman at home?"

She shook her head vigorously.

"No. He is on his way. He is annoyed you came here without telling him in advance."

"We like to talk to people if we can in their home environment, away from interruptions."

This was less than the whole truth, and no answer to her. He had got Reggie's home address from the offices of Northern Television, and then only by pulling police rank and muscle. "He likes to keep his home life separate," the secretary had said. "Don't we all," he had replied, adding, "This is a murder case. Perhaps a triple murder case. I don't think Mr. Friedman would want obstacles put in our way. Not if he's wise he wouldn't." She had caved in.

"Could I come in and wait for him?"

"Of course."

She stood aside and let him into a high hallway. Her

English was verbally perfect, but accented. She walked with him across to an open door, leading to a sitting room with tea things laid out on a low table. Orders from Reggie, Charlie thought. He sat down and she sat opposite him and pressed the switch on the electric kettle.

"Why don't we wait until your husband arrives?" Charlie said.

She shook her head.

"Reggie doesn't like tea. And yours is not a social call, is it?"

"Not really. Milk and sugar, please."

"How I like it too."

It seemed to Charlie like a shy advance.

"Your English is very good," he said, taking up his cup.

"Thank you. There was good teaching in Romanian schools. Maybe a little old-fashioned, because we were cut off for so long, but good."

"Cut off? Do you mean during the Ceauşescu years?"

"Yes. Years, you say. When I talk to older people they make it seem like an age, an eternity. Half a lifetime, with nothing happening."

"How did you meet up, you and your husband?"

"Reggie had leave from the *Terrace*. He was to make a documentary film on the Romanian orphans. That is what everyone knows about Romania, and sometimes it is the only thing."

"And what were you doing?"

"I was liaising between his crew and the Romanian television company. Also with the Romanian staff in the orphanages. It was very interesting, but also very upsetting. All of us were very much moved by what we saw."

Charlie found the faint, breaking voice moving too, though the manner was rather that of reciting a lesson.

"And did you get married over there?"

"Oh yes. We were married by the British consul in Timisoara. With some of the British cameramen as witnesses. It was very simple and very emotional."

"How do you like living in England?"

Once again the suggestion of reciting a lesson was strong.

"I am very lucky. Most of my friends in Romania would have given anything for the chance I have had. I live very well, and I learn all the time."

Charlie noticed she had not answered the question.

"And you have a child," he said.

"Yes—so lucky. A lovely boy. Perfect. And I have a little car of my own, and we can go, he and I, to Keighley or to Skipton, and I can do shopping. One day I will be able to go into Leeds, but Reggie says driving there is very, very difficult, and I am not to try it yet."

"He's quite right about that," said Charlie. He had not meant to imply that he was wrong about much else, but the little wife—what was her name? seemed to take it in that way. She leaned forward.

"He is a very good man, Reginald. You notice I call him by his big and proper name. So beautiful a name, so let others call him Reggie. In his work he has to be the big dictator, the man who takes all the important decisions. That is how it should be, otherwise chaos! But in his private life he is such a good person, so caring, so so-lic-i-tous about us. Because he loves little Ian so much. We think hard about the name, and we call him Ian so that I can think of him as Ion—a good Romanian name! He takes such good care of us, and is always so loving. Ian is so lucky, and so am I."

"I'm glad to hear—"

But Charlie was interrupted by the front door being thrown open. Reggie Friedman strode in, obviously blazing with anger, but keeping a strong control over it because he knew to let it loose on a policeman would be the height of unwisdom.

"Oh—Inspector Peace. I was told you were coming here. It was quite unnecessary. We could have talked in the studio."

"Quite. Or at the police station," said Charlie. "That is usually the best place if we want to avoid interruptions. But I thought that my purposes could best be served by talking to you at home."

"Oh," said Reggie, nonplussed. Then he pulled himself together. "You've had tea, I see. Perhaps you would leave us, Livia?"

"Of course." She got up. Charlie saw for the first time that one shoulder on her thin body was twisted, as if she had been slightly abnormal since birth, and had learned to live with it, to conceal its severity from a casual gaze. She nimbly packed up the tea things on the tray and, with a shy smile at Charlie, disappeared from the room.

"I expect you'll want to get down to this as quickly as possible," said Charlie.

"Please. I have to get back to the studio."

"I apologize for inconveniencing you, and for not getting round to talking to you earlier. Naturally with three possible intended victims of the fire, and three corpses, two of them certainly, one of them possibly, murdered, our investigation is a complex one. Who was hated so much that the murderer could adopt such a horrific and wholesale method to kill him or her?"

"And you're going on to say that only Hamish Fawley fills the bill, aren't you?" There was always something of the smart aleck about Reggie Friedman in conversation, even with a policeman.

"Yes, I was. I can't see Sylvia Cardew as anything other than unfortunate, a bit player who's been unlucky enough to fall into a major role. Bet Garrett was more generally hated, but Hamish Fawley was almost universally hated, mostly because he went out of his way to be."

"And what about Vernon Watts?"

"Also generally hated, but surely much less poisonous than Fawley, and put up with for so many years that it is difficult to see what motive there could be for getting rid of him *now*, so late in the day."

"So we'll settle on Hamish. Universally hated, as you said."

"No, I said *almost*. So far as I can tell the exception was yourself."

Reggie had seen this coming.

"There are limitations on the person who leads a team," he said, with just a slight access of pomposity. "Which is what the cast of a soap opera is. You have to exercise restraint on what you say and do, for the sake of the show."

"And did you exercise such restraints with Vernon Watts?"

"Yes . . . Oh well, not so many, perhaps. He was less poisonous as you said, and the last thing that he'd do was endanger his job on the program. He'd push me so far, and I'd flash a danger signal, and he'd draw back."

"But Hamish would not?"

"Hmmm . . . a difficult question. But not usually he wouldn't. I could imagine him pulling out of the show without filming his dying scene. That would have been just like Hamish, but not like Vernon, who would have milked a death scene for all it was worth, just to satisfy his abnormally large ego."

"Why did you have Hamish back?"

Reggie sighed.

"Haven't we been over this? The cast had been sinking into a rut. It happens in all soaps. They all hated Hamish, and they snapped out of their slump to league up against him. By having him dying of TB I assured them that the torment wouldn't last long."

"Right. Now let me put an alternative theory. Hamish had something on you, and was pressuring you to bring him back on the show."

"You can use the word 'blackmail' if you wish, Inspector. I'm not a sensitive flower."

"Right. The opportunity for you to give in to the blackmail without arousing too much comment came with Vernon Watts's death. Lots of vacant space where his sentimental friendship with the paper girl had been. So Hamish comes back. But you trick him, because he's doomed to a short life, which will end any later chances of jobs with the soap."

"I didn't trick him. I can prove that to be untrue. I

have correspondence with him in which I tell him clearly it's a short-term contract, because his character dies."

Charlie nodded, inwardly registering that the letter could have failed to be posted.

"Once he rejoined the cast," Charlie said, "there was another possibility: that he then started blackmailing you again, to get his character reprieved. A new miracle cure, perhaps? Misdiagnosis by his American doctors? That's a real possibility, because the medical setup in the U.S. is over here regarded as one degree lower than a showroom of used-car salesmen."

"We're shown in Canada, so we'd have to be careful," said Reggie, ever the professional.

"I'm sure you would go just so far, and no further."

Reggie shifted himself forward in his chair.

"You're forgetting one thing, Inspector. There is no way that Hamish saw his future as an actor in a soap. He didn't, any more than Susan and James do. You know our young love interest?"

"I know them, and know *of* them."

"Good. Then you'd know they've set their sights on the Royal Shakespeare Company or the National, or alternatively on a high-class sort of film stardom. Soaps are a real comedown for such actors' great expectations."

"But Hamish was rather different, surely? He was twenty years older than Susan and James, for a start."

"About seventeen years, actually. Oh, admittedly he wasn't putting himself forward for the young parts. But for a male actor the really meaty parts come to the older men. If James and Susan were aiming at Romeo and Juliet, Hamish would be targeting Macbeth and Othello, with King Lear to follow twenty years on. No contest who would get the better parts. No, Hamish aimed at the stars, and he was a very good actor."

"Very *good*?"

"Well, very competent, if you prefer that. But he made Cyril Wharton into a real man who happened to be homosexual, not one of your prancing parodies, spitting out every consonant."

Charlie considered this for a moment.

"You're talking as if you thought he was a very fine actor who could well have ended up in one of the big national companies."

"He was. In the RSC fine actors play Banquo and Macduff. He could have done that. Great actors play Macbeth, and that he would never do."

"But if he had these ambitions, why was he so poisonous to everybody?"

Reggie shrugged.

"Actors aren't saints, and most of them have egos well above the national average. Hamish enjoyed being beastly to people, so he was beastly to people."

"Looking at his life since he came back to the *Terrace*," said Charlie, "the two people he had most to do with on a personal level were Bet Garrett and Sylvia Cardew. Both you might say on the fringe of the prostitution trade. Sylvia most of the time well into it, but with strong ambitions to be an actress. Bet was sleeping around for a variety of reasons: as a way of getting what she wanted in the acting profession, because she enjoyed it, and probably from time to time simply for money or other favors."

"Let me interrupt you. I've never heard that Bet was

very successful at screwing—sorry!—money out of people. She was generally known to be available, and that
lowers your market value something chronic. She never
got what she wanted—a stable part in the *Terrace*. In the
main, she went sleeping around because she enjoyed it."

"Fair enough. My point was to wonder whether
Hamish made a habit of associating with people who
had a stake in the sex trade."

Reggie visibly tensed up.

"That's surely your job to find out, Inspector. My
acquaintanceship with him was almost entirely confined
to the set and the canteen."

Charlie consumed a metaphorical pinch of salt.

"But the fact that you got on fairly well with him
means that apart from Bet Garrett and Sylvia Cardew,
you will have had the most open conversations with him,
were most likely to be his confidant."

"Hamish didn't need a confidant. He was too bloody
self-confident to go around baring his heart. As a matter of
fact, I don't remember a single occasion on which he had
the sort of man-to-man talk you seem to be hinting at."

"OK—but let's assume for a moment that he was
active in the sex trade, on its grubbier edges. The likely
thing is, surely, that it was there he did something for
you, or gained knowledge of you, that he could use
against you. He left the cast first time round, presumably
he got a more prestigious job—"

"He was in London revivals of *The Second Mrs. Tan-
queray* and *School for Scandal*. Both of them were very
unhappy productions."

"I see. So the time came when it suited him to come

back to the *Terrace,* and he began to use the knowledge he'd gained a couple of years before. He still had power to hurt you. Either he would damage you personally, or he'd damage you professionally—with the company that produced the soap. Or possibly the information he had would do both."

The reply surprised him.

"It was worse," Reggie said suddenly. "Much worse. I had got married."

"Of course. You'd been in Romania."

"I had three months' leave to make a film about the Romanian orphans. That covered the time of Hamish's departure. Cyril Wharton left the *Terrace* to go to California. When I got back, with Livia, my wife, the program was a better, nicer, cleaner place to work on."

"And you had a good marriage?"

"Exactly. So in addition to my career in the soap there was my private happiness to destroy. And believe me, Hamish did enjoy destruction. He had a whole new thunderbolt he could threaten to unleash. And he would have liked nothing better."

"And yet Hamish did in the event film the death scene of Cyril Wharton."

"That was landed upon him as a complete surprise. There was really no way he could refuse, particularly when it was emphasized that this was no more than a filmed rehearsal."

"You'd planned that in advance?"

"Of course."

"So that you had something in the can that could be used to cover Cyril's death?"

"Yes."

"Another way of putting it would be that you planned to murder Hamish, but wanted to have a death scene filmed so that the soap could be broadcast as scheduled."

"I didn't murder Hamish. I'm incapable of murdering anyone."

It was said with all the spurious rectitude of school-teachers and clergymen.

"Yet you strike me as very determined, capable, decisive," said Charlie. "And I'd class such people as capable of murder, provided they were being threatened in an aspect of their lives that they hold very dear."

"That's a bit waffly, Inspector, but I get your point. I can only repeat, I'm incapable of killing anybody."

"But you were being threatened. Tell me about that."

Reggie let out a strange neigh of distress, turned in his chair away from Charlie, then took a minute or two to regain his composure, or some semblance of it. Suddenly, Charlie guessed, the fake front was falling.

"I shall deny saying this if necessary," he said, his voice wavering. "I notice you have brought no colleague with you."

"I did that for a reason," said Charlie. Reggie looked at him, hoping for elaboration, but he got nothing. He thought, then went on.

"Have you ever considered that people often fall into crime almost without knowing what they are doing? A pederast by taste who wouldn't think of abusing a child buys pretty harmless photographs of naked children, then gradually sinks into the sort of child pornography that could only be made during child abuse?"

"I suppose that's possible," said Charlie reluctantly. "With the amount of press coverage of that sort of pornography you'd think that realization would come pretty speedily these days."

"But already the man has sunk . . . I don't want to excuse myself, but just to tell you what happened and how. I have always, since I was a boy, felt a strong sympathy for all those people hideously deformed by drugs—thalidomide and so on. When I was at college I worked with them, trying to see what could be done to bring them out, make them relate to other people . . . and to me. It could have become my life's work, and it would have been good work. But I decided not to let that take me over, and to go in a more mainstream direction."

He faded into silence.

"But you found the interest was still part of you," said Charlie.

"Yes."

"And it now had a definite sexual component?"

"Yes. Why not? They were adults. Sex made them feel complete, part of the big world, belonging and participating. I felt I was doing good. Something worthwhile. I think I was right, but . . . it became—my sexual contacts with them—rather grubby. Something I was desperate to hide. Not grubby, that's the wrong word. Something worse than that: sordid."

"That sounds as if Hamish Fawley had a hand in your activities."

"Hamish was always hot on sexual tastes, always knew how to make himself useful to people of unusual sexuality. He'd made himself generally available at drama school—to members of the staff, I mean."

"Had he—what?—procured for you? Pimped?"

Reggie paused, silent for a long time. Then: "Yes."

"When was this? And what kind of people?"

"During his first stint on the *Terrace*. I was overwhelmed with work, harassed, unhappy, lonely. He found out what I wanted, and procured it for me. God help me, I was grateful."

"Who?" insisted Charlie.

"A woman brain-damaged in an accident . . . an amputee back from Iraq . . . a Down syndrome girl."

"You say girl—"

"A girl in everything except her age. She was twenty, but had a mental age of about five. But we kept within the letter of the law, wasn't that great? I insisted to Hamish that I'd have nothing to do with minors, but that episode sticks in my gullet now: a minor is what she was."

"The law has protection for the mentally retarded," said Charlie. "As I'm sure Hamish realized if you didn't. So what happened when Hamish came back to the show?"

"He used the blackmailing ploy of his 'services' in the past to do the same all over again. With the added threat of going to Livia with his tale, and with the 'evidence'— photographs I knew nothing about. Can you imagine how Livia would have felt about that?" He made a gesture with his hands toward his own back. "With *that*?"

Charlie sat there thinking long and hard.

"You're only telling me this because you have an almost perfect alibi, aren't you?" he said finally.

"And a feeling that you're well-disposed toward me, if for nothing else than as a victim of blackmail. Would you like to talk to Livia about times and phone calls and so on? Your people have been over it, but I suppose you want to go over it yet once more."

"Yes, I do. And I'll talk to the vicar, and to Sir Julian Hallowes, whom you called."

The work on the alibis had all been done by junior detectives. Reggie's had seemed about as impregnable as an alibi gets. When he had arrived back from filming in the Duke of York's it had been half past nine or so. Livia had a visit from the vicar in progress. Reggie shouted that he had to ring the chairman of Northern TV, Julian Hallowes. He was on the phone for the next ten minutes, and when he came off it he spoke to the vicar, also for about ten minutes. Charlie estimated that the petrol-soaked paper was stuffed through the letterbox of Fawley's rented house at about the time Reggie was driving up the bypass around Keighley, five minutes from home.

Not bad as alibis went.

When Livia came into the living room the bare outlines of the alibi were confirmed. Reggie had come into the house around nine thirty-five, had shouted greetings to the vicar and then gone through to his study to telephone. The door was open, so she could hear his voice, though she could not make out what he was talking about.

"He didn't pop his head round the door as he went past this room?" Charlie pressed her.

"He may have done, but I was sitting on the sofa, so I didn't see him."

"But you saw him when the phone call was over?"

"Oh yes. He came in and had a good chat with Wickham—that's the vicar. It takes about forty minutes to drive from Leeds to Keighley, and another five minutes to get here—that is if you're driving at night. I know because Reggie often rings at the end of evening filming so I can have his dinner ready. There is no way he could have done that dreadful thing in the center of Leeds and been out here by twenty-five to ten."

"It does seem unlikely," said Charlie.

"Ask the vicar. He saw him too."

And so, acting on their instructions, he stopped on his way home at the old, overlarge house by the church that was the Vicarage. He was met by Wickham Pedley, a middle-aged, self-depreciating man who obviously did not have it in him to push his way up the Anglican hierarchy.

"Ah, Mr. Peace."

"You've been warned of my approach," said Charlie, in friendly tones.

"Just this minute. Don't worry: I haven't been primed on what I should say. I haven't needed to be."

"Then perhaps you could give me your own account of the night of the twenty-seventh."

The vicar ushered Charlie through to his sermon factory.

"To get straight down to business: I was up there from about nine, talking to Livia. Lovely person—really loving and supportive of Reggie. I often go up there if I know he's shooting nights. Anyway, Reggie came in, popped his head round the door, and went off to make a phone call."

"When was this?"

"Round about half past nine, or a bit later."

"Did you see him when he popped his head round the door?"

"No. I was getting myself a drink. But I could tell by the acoustic that he was, briefly, in the room. Then I had a good talk with him when he'd finished the call."

"When was this?"

"About twenty, maybe quarter to ten."

"And what did you talk about?"

"Oh, one of our usual topics: getting Livia involved in church affairs in the village. He thinks it's too soon, though she goes to church every Sunday, so there's beginning to be comment that she doesn't help at bazaars, bring-and-buy sales, carol services. He thinks her time is taken up with looking after baby Ian. I know she has lots of time on her hands. And so on."

"He seems very . . . protective," said Charlie.

"Ah—you noticed. Frankly there is a reason, ground for this. We are a very tight-knit community. That's the polite way of putting it. Closed might be more accurate. Or inward-looking. Newcomers take ages to become accepted, if they ever are. Reggie is afraid she will be snubbed—there are a variety of unlovely ways people here do that. He's afraid she will get hurt, and since he is meditating moving closer to Leeds, for work purposes, he doesn't want Livia to go through the agony of it. And to be fair to him, they are wonderfully happy together—alone together."

"Did you hear what he was talking about to Sir Julian?"

"Oh yes—or bits of it. Sir Julian is a devotee of *Jubilee*

Terrace. Reggie tells me it's quite a joke among Northern TV employees. He was bringing him up-to-date on the plotlines in the episodes he'd filmed that week. I remember he said, 'I'll be glad to get rid of Fawley—he's poison.' Of course I know that meant he would shortly be finishing filming, when his character died. Then he said he wanted to get a firm contract for as long as possible for an Australian lad—he'd mentioned him to Sir Julian before: the one who plays a curate, very nicely, who can be promoted a bit higher if necessary. He said he was very good, and would make the first clergyman in a soap not to be a namby-pamby, milk-and-water, generally useless piece of furniture. It was rather embarrassing. I had to keep telling myself he was talking about clergymen in soaps, not in real life."

When Charlie was finished the Reverend Pedley escorted him to the door. As he was waving good-bye he shouted to Charlie opening his car door, "Remember they are in love. Deeply, genuinely, poetically in love. You don't often see it."

On the road back to Leeds, Charlie kept looking at Reggie's alibi from every angle he could think of. As far as Friedman committing the crime was concerned the alibi seemed definitely foolproof. The only possible loophole he could see would be if Reggie had commissioned someone else—someone in the cast of, or connected in some way or another with, *Jubilee Terrace* to do the killing for him. And for someone who was escaping from one blackmailer to put himself even more completely in the power of another did seem the height of improbability. It wouldn't pass as a plot ploy even in a soap.

CHAPTER 15

The Night in Question

✳

Charlie sat at his desk in the control room at Millgarth the next morning and distributed sheets of paper to DCs Rani and Hargreaves, who were facing him. When he had given them a copy each of nearly a dozen sheets he sat down and looked rather dispiritedly at the first sheet.

"These are the people who have what you might call basic alibis for the arson attack. They mostly went home when filming finished, and they have some vestiges of corroboration for what they did."

The three policemen gazed at the details. Typical was Garry Kopps, who played the corner-shop owner Arthur Bradley. Filming had finished at eight fifty, he thought. He had left the Northern TV studios five minutes later, and had arrived home around nine fifteen. He had had what he usually called his "father-sitter" waiting for him: he had paid her, they had talked for a few minutes, then she had left and he had been alone with his father. About the time the sitter had left the fire was started in Bridge Street, near the center of Leeds. It would take about twenty minutes in the evening to drive there from his home in Cookridge.

His activities were better attested to than most. Susan Fyldes, the *jeune première,* went to her flatlet in Pudsey, near the public library, and her upstairs neighbor said she heard "horrible music" from about ten or quarter past nine.

"Well, I wouldn't have expected it would be Charlotte Church or Il Divo," said Charlie.

Susan's opposite number in the young-love stakes went straight from the studio to the Lights arcade, where he was well known at the cinema and was given special concessions when he took in all or part of the big film on its last daily showing. This was not because he pleaded indigence but because the cashier was in love with his looks.

"No regular girlfriend, apparently," said Charlie.

"A bit of a loner then," said Hargreaves.

"Yes. He likes it that way, and it suits the rest of the cast as well."

Winnie Hey and Marjorie Harcourt-Smith had shared a cab to Winnie's flat in The Calls, after which it had gone on to drop Marjorie off in Headingley. Marjorie had gone to borrow milk from a neighboring flat, sometime around ten, and Winnie had put on Wagner from Covent Garden on Radio Three.

"Wagner was on that night," said Charlie, "but the fact that it was on, and audible to the neighbors (one of them used that same phrase, 'horrible music,' to describe it) did not mean that Winnie was in the flat drinking it in. I don't need to tell you how near The Calls are to Bridge Street," he concluded.

"Five minutes?" suggested Rani.

"Seven or eight with all those crossings and with Winnie's mobility problems," said Charlie. "I just can't see her as the arsonist, but that's beside the point. It was possible."

"Neither woman has a car, apparently," said Hargreaves. "We could trawl the garages to see who had a geriatric lady buying a can of petrol."

"They are not geriatric, either of them," said Charlie firmly. "You'd know that if you'd crossed them. They are both formidable and on the ball, and I'd put my money on them any day. Now, the Kerridges: both family people. Philip Marston apparently got home to his family at ten past nine and Carol Chisholm got home to hers at twenty past. All fine and dandy."

"Except that it's not," said Rani. "Going by your expression."

"No. They're a bit flimsy. Philip Marston has three children. The oldest—nineteen, from a first marriage—is at Bradford University, and was at kung fu classes that evening. The two younger ones, from this present marriage, are five and three, and were in bed. So Marston's alibi depends on his wife."

"Not ideal. What about Chisholm? Nice lady, or so she looks on TV."

"So she is, I've no doubt," said Charlie. "However, her family consists of one son, out till eleven, and one sixteen-year-old daughter currently going through teenage rebellion at its most obstructionist. She is these days in a constant state of rage with her mother. Refuses to say when her mother got home, says she wasn't sure but she thought it was nearly ten."

Hargreaves sighed.

"Don't we all know it? You'll be going through it before long, sir. That girl of yours is a terror in the making."

"Was. Past tense. Now that she's got a small brother she's a changed character."

"Off your back and on to his, I suppose."

"Exactly. I'll have to give him some tuition. Into what *not* to do, of course. Anyway, that's a pretty shaky alibi too."

"What about her husband?"

"Down at the pub. Supposed to be adolescent-sitting, but was persuaded by the teenage Che Guevara to go down for a quick one. Didn't get back till ten fifteen."

They all nodded their heads.

"Which leaves us," said Charlie, riffling his papers, "with Les Crosby the newsagent (wife to vouch for him), the two backroom boys Reggie and Melvin, and Stephen Barrymore. Reggie we discussed last night in the canteen: we decided he's out unless he employed a hit man or woman."

"Difficult to imagine, as you said," said Rani.

"Melvin Settle has about the best of the alibis," said Charlie. "At home with his wife and a houseful of children and their pals. So we can more or less rule him out—"

"Except for the same proviso as with Friedman," said Hargreaves.

"He could offer a really good story line in return for having the job done," said Rani.

"And looking at one or two of the actors, they'd be his for a couple of strong scenes," said Charlie. "Though I don't know about you, but I wouldn't make actors my first choice if I was recruiting a hit man. OK, though: we'll keep the possibility in mind."

"What about the Merry Divorcée?" asked Rani. "Where was she on the night?"

"Drinking in an impromptu and probably illegal bar in the Otley Road Guesthouse (if you don't know it, you haven't missed anything). That's an alibi worth looking at: Were there any other guests or friends of the owner there, and was Bet Garrett really there the whole evening as she says, or were there blank periods when she slipped away? Then there's the new boy, Stephen Barrymore. He's everybody's favorite youngster on the set. Good theatrical name too, so Felicity tells me."

"I can't think of any stage actors called Barrymore," said Hargreaves.

"Before even your time," said Charlie. "Whole family of them. Best known was John—all the star parts on the American stage between the wars. Sloshed to the eyeballs most of the time. They all seem to be welcoming young Stephen as if he's going to be a typical Barrymore and double the ratings."

"Have you looked at your contract?" Melvin asked Stephen Barrymore, on the set of *Jubilee Terrace,* where Stephen was filming a nice scene in which he comforted Winnie Hey in her bereavement.

"Yes. Went through it last night. Seems fine. Of course I'd need to consider anything else that could be in the offing."

"You're committed to *Emmerdale* for three weeks' filming. After that we'd want you here full-time."

"Of course I understand that. But there's the question of dosh—"

Melvin waved his hand.

"Take that up with the financial powers that be. But take my word for it: you won't get more from them than you will from us. And you get thirty percent more viewers with us, imprinting your beguiling image on the wall of their brains, assuming that they've got any."

"Still, I need to look at—"

"Take my advice: start haggling when you have a distinct and likeable image in the public mind to use as your bargaining chip. By the way, I think we'll have you lodging with Marjorie."

Stephen looked gobsmacked.

"But I've got a flat in Leeds. In Stanningley—that's not far. I don't need to be bloody chaperoned—"

"Stephen, I'm talking about *Jubilee Terrace*. Kevin Plunkett the curate will move in with Gladys Porter the lonely widow. There could even be battles over you between her and Lady Wharton. They might be a nice respite from the serious stuff."

Stephen Barrymore looked shamefaced.

"Oh, er, right. I get you."

Actually he looked relieved.

"You're already getting the usual disease of actors in soaps," said Melvin Settle.

"Which is?"

"Not knowing when you are the bloke in the soap and when you are the bloke in the real world."

"You ought to do what I do."

The voice, from behind Melvin's shoulder, was that of Young Foulmouth.

"I hardly think so," said Stephen, sounding positively archepiscopal.

"Keep putting 'fucking' and 'cunt' into sentences when I'm being myself, *not* when I'm being Jason Worseley."

"Well, well," said Stephen. "There's method in your scurrility, is there?"

"Too right there is, cobber."

"Well, I'm afraid my parents taught us not to swear or utter blasphemy."

"'Bout time you kicked over the fucking traces. When you're being Stephen you can knee your other self in the balls. When you mention God you can say 'if the old bugger exists at all' or 'fucking sadist that he is.'"

"You know, I don't think I like the idea. I think when I'm being the real me I won't mention God at all."

"That would put you on a par with most of the clergymen I know," said Melvin Settle.

"After filming," said Charlie, "Stephen Barrymore went to a party held at the College of Drama and Music, where he's still officially a student. He was the center of attention, of course—the girls mad about him, full of admiration at his getting a real acting job in that dramatic way, the boys mad at him because they're jealous as hell. Stephen lapped it up—the shape of things to come."

"He's a good-looking lad," said Hargreaves. "I should think he's pretty used to it already."

"Ah, but now with money attached," said Charlie. "As the poet says 'How pleasant it is to have money, have money, How pleasant it is to have money.'"

"Doesn't sound like any poet I've ever read," said Hargreaves.

"You haven't read any," said Charlie.

"When did he get to the party?" asked Rani.

"About half past nine," Charlie said, after consulting his sheets of reports. "He had a taxi called from Reception at the studio because the rank outside was empty. We haven't checked with the drivers, but timewise it all hangs together. We'd have to learn a great deal more about things happening between him and Hamish before he could become a serious suspect . . . Which brings us to Bill Garrett . . ."

They all looked at one another.

"The prime suspect as far as I'm concerned," said Hargreaves.

"And you've done a driving experiment," prompted Charlie. "Tell us."

"Right." Hargreaves expanded his extensive self in his small chair. "The Red Deer—you both know it—is a pub at the top of Briggate—junction with Merrion Street. There's a parking area, a municipal one half a minute away, which gets crowded if there's something popular on at the Grand Theatre, but otherwise is pretty quiet on weekday evenings. If he parked there when he and Liza Croome went for their drink and heart-to-heart he could have left the Red Deer, got into his car, driven up North Street, down Byron Street, and into Bridge Street. Matter of three and a half minutes by my calculation. Petrol and newspapers in the boot: out with them, stuff them through the letterbox, set the last one alight. Two minutes. Back in the car and off via Eastgate and Briggate. Under ten minutes."

He sat back, pleased with himself.

"Premeditation then," said Rani.

"What do you mean?"

"Having the newspapers and petrol in the boot."

Hargreaves considered.

"Plenty of people have a can of petrol in case of emergencies, and pile up their newspapers in the boot for when they get to a recycling point."

"Agreed," said Charlie. He shuffled his pile of papers. "Who talked to him about his alibi, and who checked it?"

"Dick Fallon," said Hargreaves gloomily.

"OK. Not the brightest sparkler in the packet. We'll talk to the staff at the Red Deer, then get Bill Garrett in, or go and talk to him. Check if he's at the studios, Rani, and we'll assume he's at home if he's not."

"At last, some action," said Hargreaves.

"Do you think the police will come, Dad?" asked Angela Garrett, home for lunch and unpacking and repacking her schoolbag for the afternoon.

"How do I know, darling? They took down what I was doing when the fire started. Perhaps that satisfied them. Liza, the landlord, and ten or fifteen others saw me at the pub. It should be enough."

"Dad, the chap who talked to you about the alibi was just a junior, the one who did all the donkey work. And he was pretty much of a donkey himself. The top man is the black one. He's starting to interview the prime suspects, so everybody says."

"Don't use silly jargon like 'prime suspects.' Leave it to the TV scriptwriters. And 'everybody' means the children at school whose parents are in *Jubilee Terrace*, I suppose?"

"Well, yes. But don't get all snotty. And we're not all 'children,' those of us with parents in the show."

"No. At least you're not. You've never had the chance to be a child."

Angela, standing at the window, was shaking her head.

"No sign of a police car."

"Oh, for heaven's sake, Angela. Detective Inspector Peace will come in an unmarked car. When he comes, if he comes. Get off to school, my girl."

"Bye, Dad."

She ran out the door and down the stairs. Bill worried that she hadn't half enough clothes on for a chilly October day.

"I talked to your young chap," said the landlord of the Red Deer. "What's the matter? Did he make a muddle of it? I didn't get the impression he was a brain of Britain."

"We always try to go over things twice," said Charlie patiently. "You'd be surprised how many new things people come up with the second time around."

"Well, you won't get any new things from me," the landlord said firmly. "I've reviewed it in my own mind since, and all I told that young feller-me-lad was true, and it was everything I noticed about them."

"OK," said Charlie, nodding to Rani to take notes. "What time did they arrive?"

The landlord sighed.

"Bloody hell—oh, all right. Hold your horses. It was ten past nine, maybe a bit after: quarter past, let's say. Business pretty slow, so I served them straightaway, and they went and sat over there." He pointed to the remotest part of the bar.

"Did you see where they parked their car?"

"Fer Christ's sake . . . I'm behind this bar when I'm not collecting glasses. I don't care where they park their . . . cars."

"Did you get any impression about Garrett's frame of mind?"

"Yes, I did. I got the impression that he was thirsty after a long filming session."

Charlie sighed. A humorist.

"So he and his lady friend started talking."

"'Course they did. It's what they came for, isn't it? They sat, bent forward, talking in low voices. Doesn't mean they were planning to murder anybody. If you ask me—"

"I didn't," said Charlie, losing his patience.

"—it was the British National Party or some of the other racist groups that did it. It's what they do, set fire to houses. They just got the wrong house."

"Nobody from the minorities lives in those houses in Bridge Street," said Charlie.

"Then they got the wrong bloody street, didn't they?"

"Now, while they were here, did Bill Garrett leave the bar for a while?"

The landlord gave one of his sighs.

"I'm here to serve drinks. Most people in this bar drink beer of some sort. It means they often go to the loos. I've got better things to think about than 'Oh my, Bill Garrett has gone to the gents' or 'why, now Liza Croome has gone to the ladies'.' I just don't notice things like that . . . One of the customers said he did, though."

"Oh." The three men were immediately alert. "Who?"

"Pete Savage. Comes Monday and Thursday evenings, regular as clockwork."

"Where did he see Bill Garrett?"

"In the car park."

"Was he getting into or out of his car?"

"Neither. He was just standing some way away."

"Smoking? On his mobile? Talking to anyone?"

"You'd have to talk to him. People do go out there to have a smoke now and then, what with these new regulations and so on. But I don't remember Garrett as a smoker, even when it was legal."

"Nobody else saw him out there?"

"Not so far as I know."

There was no point in keeping the landlord any longer from his life's vocation.

"Happy?" Rani asked, when he and Charlie stood in the parking area.

"Not entirely," said Charlie. "We've got Bill Garrett at the pub, and we've got him out here. Where we haven't got him is at number nine Bridge Street. But it'll have to do for the moment."

They looked at each other, resisted the thought of having a pint, then went about their business.

CHAPTER 16

Those Responsible

✳

Charlie Peace saw the figure of a teenage girl disappearing around the end of the road in the St. Catherine's School uniform of green check blouse and dark green worsted skirt. He was well up on the names and identities of the remaining members of the Garrett household, and he congratulated himself on arriving just at the right time. Hargreaves had been called out to a domestic, but Rani was still with him. They got on well together, with a similar approach to knotty problems: theoretic without being cold. They usually found they were thinking along the same lines, without needing to put into words what those lines were.

Bill Garrett was welcoming when he opened the door, without being positively friendly. Exactly calculated and just right, Charlie thought. Trust an actor.

"I've been expecting you," said Bill, refraining from adding: "What took you so long?"

"I like to clear away the little byways and irrelevancies first," said Charlie, sensing the query. "You don't need me to tell you that you're fairly central to our inquiry, or seem to be, considering your bad relationship with your wife and her recent taking-up with Hamish Fawley."

Bill gestured toward the threadbare armchair and sofa, but made no offer of coffee or tea.

"My relationship, as you call it, with Bet has improved a lot since she gave up her claims to the children. And nobody ever believed her proposed marriage to Fawley was going to come off."

"Mr. Garrett," said Charlie gently, "you're talking about the present. What we know, or think we know, *now* is that both of them were playing a sort of sadistic game with you and the children. But I don't think that's what anyone knew *then*, three days ago, when the fire was started. And I don't think it's what you thought then either."

The actor's confident taking-up of positions, which Charlie had noticed, seemed already to be shaking, he did not know why. Bill thought for several seconds, then all he could come up with was, "Yes. Well—I don't know—was it different then?"

"You must know it was. Everything I've heard from other members of the cast of *Jubilee Terrace* suggests that you believed in the engagement, believed in the battle for custody of the children. Probably you thought the two went together; the engagement was designed to strengthen the custody bid."

"You're exaggerating," said Bill, inclining toward bluster. "I don't think I took it that seriously. We none of us did. Why would Bet genuinely want custody when she bitterly resented ever having to put herself out for the girls? She knew how demanding custody of the girls would be if she took her duties seriously."

Charlie was silent for a moment, digesting his words.

"I think you more than most have reason to know the answer to your question why she would want this custody. She is an emotional sadist. The marriage had collapsed long ago, but since she could no longer torment you with her flagrant unfaithfulness she could use the children to get at you. Your weak point was that you loved them, where she was totally indifferent if not actually hostile. They made wonderful tools to hurt you, and she had no scruples or tender feelings to stop her using them."

"Maybe. I suppose so. She is a terrible woman."

"You see, we have to be interested in what the situation was at the time of the double murder. You thought the engagement was still on."

"I think everybody did," said Bill, changing his story much too rapidly.

"I agree. I heard her say that it had been broken off days before the murder, but she and Hamish had decided to say nothing about it. That being so, it was a fair bet that your wife and Hamish would still be sharing the house in Bridge Street the night of the murder. You'd kill two birds with one stone."

"Nasty image. I'd nothing against Hamish Fawley."

"Everyone had something against Hamish Fawley."

"Nothing particular. Just that he was a nasty-tongued troublemaker."

"I bet the last thing you'd want was him as stepfather to your children, with constant access to them."

There was silence. Then Bill said with some dignity, "I

would have hated it. But I didn't think there was any chance it would happen." He then, to Charlie's surprise, added, "And by the way I had nothing against Vernon Watts either."

Charlie shrugged.

"Oh, I think we can say that Watts is an irrelevancy. I've always thought so. He fell in front of a bus, after a heart attack, but since he was disliked people amused themselves by talking about possible murder. This was taken up when another murder—a real murder—was being planned, to make it look as if *Terrace* actors were being targeted. A real red herring, but with one interesting aspect."

"What was that?"

"That the arson was decided and prepared for well in advance. We know that because of the anonymous letter that was sent to the police."

"I see." Bill's voice sounded glum. His early access of confidence was now largely evaporated.

"Now," said Charlie, "after the filming on the night in question, you and Liza Croome went for a drink in the Red Deer, is that right?"

"Why not?"

"I'm not criticizing. But it is nowhere near the Northern TV studios."

"Have you tried the pubs that are?"

"Fair enough. But you chose one within easy driving distance of Bridge Street."

"Practically all the pubs in Leeds center are that."

"Not the ones in the pedestrianized parts. And the Red Deer has a small Council parking area just above it."

"So?"

"It was easy for you to go outside for a cigarette, or to make a phone call, then to jump into your car, go and do the necessary, then be back within ten minutes."

"Except that I never thought of it. Ask Liza if the car was in a different position when we left the park to go to our homes."

"No reason why it should be. There is usually very little doing up there before people come out of the theaters and clubs, plenty of open parking places."

"Setting fire to a house needs preparation."

"Not much. You probably keep old newspapers in the boot till you go to a recycling skip. You may be one of the people who keep a bit of petrol in the boot, against emergencies."

"I don't."

"So you say. Easy enough to buy a can on the way to the studios to film. Then all you have to do is say, 'I'm going to the loo,' nip outside, and jump into the car."

"So have you got someone who saw me 'jump' into the car?"

"We have someone who saw you in the parking area."

"Doing what? Standing around or making a phone call, I bet."

"He saw you standing around, yes."

"Seems like I wasn't in much of a hurry, doesn't it? I think if I was going to do it at all I'd have 'jumped' straight into the car and driven off to do it."

Charlie felt he had been trumped on one of his best cards. Worse, he felt that Bill, by getting these points across, was gaining a new source of confidence.

"You mentioned phoning," he said.

"Because that's what I did. I phoned my daughters to see if they were all right."

"And were they?"

"Yes. I spoke to the eldest. She was waiting in the pizza takeaway we go to. She'd been too busy to cook anything for their supper, so she thought they needed something more substantial."

"And what time was this?"

"Twenty past nine? Half past, twenty to ten? It's not the sort of thing you remember. Angela will vouch for me."

"But she can't vouch for where you were, can she? You and your mobile could have been anywhere."

"We weren't. We were in the little car park, where your witness doubtless saw me."

Charlie was beginning to feel not so much trumped as checkmated. Luckily at this point Rani made one of his occasional forays.

"How long have you and your wife been married, Mr. Garrett?"

"Longer than I care to remember. Say fifteen years."

"You would know her habits, then?"

"I suppose you mean her sexual habits, don't you?" Bill said. "They're a distant memory."

"I just wondered why the murderer assumed that she and Hamish would be in bed at half past nine."

"That's a matter for the police. I don't need to explain why I was no expert in Hamish and Bet's habits. I wasn't interested, and I have no ambitions to play Peeping Tom."

"Any cases of arson I've been on—racial ones usually,

admittedly—the fire has been set at a later hour when everyone in the house is asleep."

"And this one wasn't? As I say, it's a matter for the police. Could it be that the arsonist saw the lights were turned off?"

"What were you wearing on the night in question, sir?"

"Wearing? Good Lord, I don't know."

"You'd just been filming, sir."

"Then it would be . . ." Bill had to think hard. ". . . It would have been one of Bob Worseley's standard outfits. Bartending clobber, from the wardrobe. I think it was a shirt—big check, rough-looking—flannels, loud socks."

"What did you do with them after filming finished?"

"Nothing. I went home in them. That's usual with evening filming. Then I took back the whole outfit next day, or the next time I went to the studios."

"Which was?"

Bill frowned in concentration. "Yesterday, actually."

"It was a cold night, the night of the fire. Didn't you wear something else to go home in?"

"Oh, I had my usual old mac in the dressing room. I think I had that on."

"I see." Charlie looked at his watch and went over to the window. "Ah, the team is arriving."

"Team? What team?"

"Mr. Garrett, I have a warrant to search this house. I asked the team to be here at three o'clock, and they will conduct the search, supervised by me."

"And what are you looking for?"

"You won't expect me to answer that, sir. We may have

to take items for further investigation. If so I will give you a receipt."

"Big of you," said Bill. Charlie was surprised that by now the man was very relaxed, or apparently so. It was almost as if the new stage in the investigation was in the nature of a relief for Bill. As if he wanted to be deemed guilty.

Bill Garrett listened to the noises from around the living room, where he had been left in the company of a uniformed constable, and also from upstairs, where he could sense big footsteps in the various children's bedrooms, and also in the one that until recently had been nominally Bet's. Not much left there to interest anybody. He nodded when the footsteps there ceased. He had vetoed attempts by Debbie to move into the room, saying it was "too soon," so there was only stuff that Bet did not think it worth taking with her.

On the ground floor he registered the opening of the door of the clothes cupboard. Macs, overcoats, some school clothing, umbrellas, and heavy boots. He was not surprised when Inspector Peace came in, obviously having just sniffed at the old mac he was holding in his hand.

"Is this yours, sir?"

"Of course it is. It's a man's mac. I'm the only man in the house."

"These things are often unisex these days."

"Maybe. That mac's at least fifteen years old. I've done everything you can imagine in it, and a great deal besides. I've even made love in it, long, long ago. If you smell anything interesting on it, the smell could have been there for a decade and more."

Charlie smiled noncommittally and left the room again.

Bill looked at the constable, who looked back, his eyes in neutral.

"All right if I write a note to my kids?"

"Why would you want to do that, sir?"

"In case you take me in for questioning."

"Nobody's said anything about that yet."

"If they don't, I'll tear it up."

"There's nothing against it, provided we can read it as well."

"Oh, you can read it."

He sat down at the desk. Outside he heard the metal doors of his garage scraping over the concreted driveway. He took out a sheet of notepaper and wrote.

Darlings,

I'm going to the police station to answer questions. It's only a matter of routine. I've been expecting this, as it's possible whoever set the fire was aiming at your mother. *Don't worry*—I'm sure I'll see you soon. If I have to stay in overnight I know you can rely on Angela, as always. Remember, anything I do, I do for you all.

Love you all so much.
Your Dad.

He beckoned the constable over and handed it to him. The young man read, then read it again, apparently

memorizing it. Then he handed it back without comment. Bill remained sitting at the desk, lost in thought.

Traces of petrol on the mac were not much in the
way of proof. Still, they'd probably be able to prove they
were recent. The petrol would probably have got on other
items of clothing—shirt, trousers. Bill remained deep in
thought on that question. Again he was interrupted by
Charlie.

"We have only found one mobile phone, sir."

"We only have one telly—so what? We're a modest
family, Inspector."

"You phoned your daughter from outside the Red
Deer."

"Oh yes, the children have one. What child doesn't? I
should think Angela has got it on her."

"Taken it with her to school, sir?"

"Precisely. It's called a *mobile* phone. That's its
appeal."

"Thank you for pointing that out, sir."

Bill sat on. He was remembering his boxing days, when
he punched his way through drama school. In his mind
he'd always had a series of positions—possible outcomes
of fights. Position One, the optimum outcome, was an
early KO of his opposition. This was a result he very rarely
accomplished. He was rather afraid he was vacating Position One already in the fight with Inspector Peace. He'd
scored points, but that was a sign foreshadowing longer
fights. There was no sign of Peace giving up the struggle
or declaring him free from suspicion. Positions Two and
Three were a late KO and a victory on points, and both

possibilities, less desirable than the first, were becoming the ones to aim for. Position Four, his own defeat, had been a frequent result in his boxing matches, suffered with equanimity and good humor, but they were not something he could bear to contemplate in this contest.

"We're very nearly finished here," said Charlie, coming back. The constable gestured toward the letter on the desk, and Charlie read through it, concentrating. "Yes, that will be all right," he said. "I'm going to ask you some questions and it may take us some time. Is there anyone you could ask to come here and take care of your daughters when they come home from school?"

"Oh, Angela does that. But you could phone Northern TV and get them to ask Liza Croome to come over."

The five minutes in the unmarked car left Bill feeling gutted and unable to think things through. He had seen the neighbors lingering in their front gardens or behind their windows. Unmarked cars didn't fool them. He sat, his brain apparently quiescent, nonfunctioning, grappling with none of the terrible decisions facing him. When they got to Millgarth, Charlie handed him over to a uniformed constable and told him they'd be ready to question him "in an hour or so's time." He was led away to a stark, square box with a bunk and nothing else in it. Bill looked around him at the bare cream walls and wondered why they were not scrawled with the hopeless appeals of people shut up here, waiting for questioning.

The shirt. That was the vital thing. The fact that traces of petrol would be on the wrong shirt, and no traces would be on the one that should bear them, was crushing. He had held the petrol can in the way he felt sure it would have been held—hidden by the mac, leaving traces on it, and also on the shirt. The wrong shirt because it was two days later than the fire. That in itself would surely lead the policeman to the right conclusion.

Then there was the mobile phone, the third mobile. Probably Debbie's, though Rosie had one too. It was the one that had the recording of the pizza takeaway on it—the one that was played to form a background to the voice of his eldest. It was unmistakably the pizza joint they patronized, fifteen minutes' walk away from Bridge Street. As Bill had talked with Angela on the night of the fire he had recognized the voice of one of the regular customers, giving his order, his unchanging order of "one margherita, one pepperoni, and one chicken and prawn." It was a genial chap called Stan Outhwaite. Bill had talked to him often while they both waited for their orders to be ready. But the fire was on Monday, and Stan (unchanging in everything) only came to the pizzeria on a Saturday.

Which was when he had been recorded. When Bill heard the unmistakable voice and the unmistakable order, in the little car park near the Red Deer, he had been puzzled, disturbed. It was only a couple of days after the fire, when he and his eldest and favorite daughter had been discussing the death over breakfast, that Angela had looked at him searchingly, with that disturbing look of childish innocence she still had, and said, "I met him, you know. After school one day, when I was in Briggate, on the way to Marks and Spencer's. She introduced him to me. She said, 'This is my new bloke. We're going to get married and look after you lot. You need a strong bloke in your lives. Hamish will teach you all he knows.' And they both went off laughing—loud and horrible. He was a horrible man. He disgusted me." That was when Bill had gone to her wardrobe and smelled her blouse. That was the day when he'd taken her school coat out to Bramley Fall Woods and set fire to it. That was when he carried a can of petrol under his mac to take on himself the burden of guilt. It was the least he could do.

But he hadn't thought it through. He'd thought that any old shirt would do to wear, but because he'd been filming it had to be the one from the Northern TV wardrobe department. It worked both ways: that shirt, if his confession was true, should have been stained, and wasn't. The old shirt he had worn shouldn't have been stained, and was.

He thought about his attempt to take on himself the guilt as a reparation to his daughters for the awful childhood they had had. And in particular to Angela, who had assumed so many of the burdens of motherhood at a time when she was still only a child herself. The other girls had accepted Bet as she was or seemed, had even found her rather fun. Rosie had told him that. Only Angie had seen Bet for what she really was: a moral leper who blighted everything and everyone she touched. Angie comprehended that, allied with Hamish, Bet would have infected the whole brood.

He worried about Angie. He felt uneasily that she was already corrupted.

She had written the anonymous letter to the police, days before the murder, to connect it quite falsely with the natural death of Vernon Watts. She had recorded the scene at the pizza takeaway the previous Saturday knowing from Bill's schedule that he was filming on Monday, and knowing if he had evening filming he would ring her afterward if he went, as he always did after a long day's filming, for a drink.

It was the forethought, the amount of planning, that worried Bill. He would have been much happier if the murder had been the result of an adolescent explosion of rage, of an outburst of indignation at the adult responsibilities that she had had to shoulder as a result of Bet's self-absorption. The degree of planning, the cold preparation, suggested a deep infection, a corruption planted and nourished in Angela by her resentment of the burdens she carried.

Bill shook his head. Angie had always been the one child to fix her eyes on the middle distance, to foresee possible danger points and harms. Why should he diagnose corruption in her? She had always done what she needed to do to protect the younger ones. From the moment she had seen Bet and Hamish together she resolved to take preventative measures, spurred on by Bet's threat that Hamish would teach the girls "all he knew." She had only been doing what experience taught her to do.

Bill squared his shoulders. He needed to take detailed account of his current situation. The early KO—represented in his mind by the cessation of police interest in him and his family—was not going to happen. That also took care of Position Two, the late KO—the possibility that Peace was going to let investigations slide even if he had strong suspicion who the murderer was. Inspector

Peace, Bill thought, was a specimen of true and long-lasting tenacity. But there was still a hope that he could hold the line at Position Three: a hope that Peace, for all his suspicions, would compromise, possibly on orders from on high, by taking him up on his own confession of guilt. He had done what he could to make this position credible. He had held with his bare hands the can of petrol he had always kept in the garage, had held it against his mac and shirt. The wrong shirt . . . But then perhaps if he talked to Liza he could persuade her to say . . .

No. He could not involve anyone else in the terrible mess that Angie's actions had landed them all in. If he confessed, he wanted to be believed, not found not guilty, with all the consequences for Angie that would bring.

He was getting up to do the only thing that varied the monotony of sitting on the bed—walking around the room—when the door opened and Peace came in.

"Oh, at last," said Bill. "I don't see what is taking so long. I'm quite ready now to confess."

"Really?" said Peace, raising his eloquent eyebrows. "Tell me, is this by previous agreement with your daughter Angela?"

"No! Of course not! Why do you ask that?"

"Because your daughter Angela has just come into the station to confess."

It was what Bill feared most. His eyes filled with tears.

"Don't believe her! It's just Angela—she's like that: takes the responsibility for everything. She's trying to save me."

"We've had a preliminary talk," said Charlie, not sitting down but looking Bill straight in the eye, "and she's told

240

me all the details and how I can acquire concrete evidence
for the trial: petrol stains on her school blouse and the
coat—the coat that you took away and burned—the fact
of the mobile phone with the recording from the pizza
takeaway to use to convince you that's where she was on
the night—and so on."

"This is all nonsense. Silly playacting."

But he looked at the floor, which had nothing to it to
deserve looking at.

"Is it playacting? I've already established by watching
the rushes at Northern TV that your shirt that had the
traces of petrol on it was not the one you were wearing
that night. If I were to arrest you on the basis of a confession you made now, I'd have to release you in a couple of
days because the evidence would prove to be phony. I'd
have to arrest your daughter, because her evidence would
prove to be the real McCoy. I think you should sit down,
sir."

Looking dazed, Bill Garrett sat down on the bed. Suddenly he said, "They were worthless, you know—totally
worthless. Two of the most contemptible people on this
earth. No one will miss or regret them."

"But did you know Sylvia Cardew?"

"No. I was thinking of—"

"Of your wife, of course. You could be right about her
and Fawley, but in the police we're a bit like the Church.
No one is beyond redemption. So a real little Hitler is as
important to us as a Mother Teresa. What you should be
doing, sir, is not burdening us with an impossible confession. You should be thinking how to get your daughter
through this."

"But . . . what can I do? She'll be sent away—to some sort of juvenile jail, I suppose."

"I imagine so. If the evidence holds up. They're not all terrible places. Most of them are better than the regular jails. She can get an education there, helped by you from the outside, and perhaps by her school, if they will cooperate. Then there's her defense. You'll have to emphasize her motherly role in the household, the negligence of her real mother, the fake engagement that was devised just to drive you and the girls mad with fear . . ."

Charlie sat down on the other end of the bunk. The two men were no longer policeman and suspect or policeman and witness. They were, against all regulations, father and father.

About the Author

✳

ROBERT BARNARD's most recent novel is *Last Post*. Among his many other books are *The Graveyard Position*, *A Cry from the Dark*, *The Mistress of Alderley*, *The Bones in the Attic*, *A Murder in Mayfair*, *No Place of Safety*, *The Bad Samaritan*, and *A Scandal in Belgravia*. Scribner released a classic edition of his *Death of a Mystery Writer* in 2002. He is the winner of the Malice Domestic Award for Lifetime Achievement and the prestigious Nero Wolfe Award, as well as the Anthony, Agatha, and Macavity awards. An eight-time Edgar nominee, he is a member of Britain's distinguished Detection Club, and in May 2003, he received the Cartier Diamond Dagger Award for lifetime achievement in mystery writing. He lives with his wife, Louise, and their pets, Peggotty and Durdles, in Leeds, England.